THE WRONG MAN

MYDWORTH MYSTERIES #7

Neil Richards • Matthew Costello

RED DOG
UK

Published by RED DOG PRESS 2021

Originally published as an eBook edition by Bastei Lübbe
AG, Cologne, Germany, 2020.

Edited by Eleanor Abraham
Cover Design by Oliver Smyth

ISBN 978-1-913331-16-0

www.reddogpress.co.uk

1.

LAST ROUNDS

POLICE CONSTABLE BERT LOXLEY made his way slowly past the locked gates of St Thomas's Church, down Church Street, past Mydworth Motors, taking his time as he did his nightly rounds. This walk through the village was a regular-as-clockwork duty, to make sure that everything was as peaceful and quiet as could be, checking all the businesses properly shut up, windows closed, shutters down.

Behind him now, he heard the church clock strike the half hour: he paused for a second, and checked his pocket watch out of habit. *Spot on.*

Right now, the streets were empty – his shadow the only movement under the gas lamps.

Truth was, he'd hardly seen a soul tonight, though that wasn't surprising: a cold mist lingered in the damp November streets, and he could feel the chill even through his heavy uniform and mackintosh.

As he turned back and went down the High Street, his footsteps echoed on the pavement.

Yes, peaceful and quiet.

Though this night had not started that way. A call to the station about a few patrons down at the Station Inn, fuelled by one too many, who might be heading into a proper fist fight.

Which would have been the most activity that he had faced so far in the two weeks of his new posting to Mydworth – save for a lone domestic problem that had ended with the couple, blubbering in each other's arms, all suddenly forgiven. That is, Loxley knew, until the next row.

Tonight however, when he'd pitched up at the pub, the men involved had genuinely seemed to be on the edge of spilling out into the streets for a bare-knuckle battle.

But, as it turned out, simply by his walking in the door, the men seemed to freeze, neither of them clearly fancying the idea of a night cooling off in jail.

All Loxley had to do was ask: "Everything all right, gentlemen?" and the flushed faces had softened, glaring eyes lowered – and suddenly trouble had been averted.

Loxley had considered taking their names, mostly as an added bit of encouragement to finish their beers and head home quietly.

But with the grievances apparently fading – and the last round looming anyway – he didn't think it warranted taking matters further. He'd jotted a couple of names in his notebook, wished the publican a good night, and headed back up Station Road into town.

Now, as Loxley turned to go down the High Street, he looked in through the windows of the Green Man, which he'd been told was the most civilised of the town's watering holes.

The landlord wiping down the pumps, just a couple of regulars finishing up at the bar, and a handful of others, coats on, last farewells before dispersing to their homes.

For a moment he stood there, just taking in the evening: the warm camaraderie of the townsfolk leaving the warm, yellow light of the pub and heading to their cosy homes.

Mydworth. Such a *tidy* little town, Loxley thought. More like a village. And he wondered, being honest with himself, how long he would be satisfied with the sleepy ebb and flow of life here.

Life in the Metropolitan Police in London would be much more to his taste. *Plenty* of crimes to deal with, and Loxley knew that the Met had to be exploring the very latest methods of solving all sorts of cases.

But here, Sergeant Timms had been quick to inform the new constable on his first day at the station: *"We do things the old-fashioned way, Loxley. Methods that stand the test of time."*

Except, Loxley guessed, Timms' "methods" probably didn't get tested on a regular basis.

But the world was changing, growing more complex every day. People wanting different things, peacetime life not bringing everyone the peace or prosperity they had expected. Or been promised by the politicians.

And tonight – brisk, a chilly November night as if winter was in rehearsal, Mydworth remained sleepy and safe.

FINALLY – CROSSING THE SQUARE, past the Town Hall and the bank, all secure, to Hill Lane – Loxley scanned the quiet side streets, the nearby small shops shuttered, most homes now dark. *Early to bed being very much an adage held close by many in this little town, even on a Saturday night.*

He'd soon be done. Time to return to the station where that, too, would quickly go dark.

THE WRONG MAN

Any rare late-night summons would be directed to Timms at home, who would – for any significant matter – come and roust Loxley from the single room that he rented above the gentlemen's outfitters.

Halfway down Hill Lane, past the shops now, and just at the point where the street lights came to an end, he took his usual left turn into Slip-Knot Alley. This oft-used shortcut led up to the football pitch and a line of tumbledown cottages at the edge of the town which marked the end of his rounds.

What was it, the locals called these alleyways?

Ah yes, "twittens", that was it.

He unclipped his torch from his belt, turned it on: the pale beam of light catching swirls of mist on the pathway ahead.

His own steps echoed as he walked down the serpentine lane, a wall of brick on both sides.

This *twitten* must, he imagined, be a favoured spot for the young couples of the town, seeking a few minutes hidden away from prying eyes.

Wouldn't be surprised if I stumble upon something like that, even on a chilly night like this.

Then, as if in answer, the narrow lane curved for its final time, revealing a grassy opening, neatly surrounded on the side by thick bushes.

And Constable Loxley saw something in the cone of light from his torch.

FOR A MOMENT he froze, thinking that what was ahead, curled up on the grass, might be the romantic pair he'd been imagining previously.

But no. Loxley immediately knew what the shape must be.

Of course. Some fellow heading home from the pub, using this as a shortcut, must have stumbled and decided a few minutes of a chilly snooze was exactly what the doctor ordered.

Before he got to the person, Loxley cleared his throat, to give the chap some warning.

"All right then. Having a spot of trouble, are we? Best you try to—"

Loxley expected the man to stir at the loud voice, giving it the heft that a request from the authorities *should* bring.

But this person – nothing.

Loxley moved closer, now – with the air growing chillier by the moment – even a bit concerned for the fellow.

"Now c'mon then, my lad. Time you were off home, time to get up."

At that, Loxley gave the back of the man's shoes a little kick. Just a small "tap, tap", a last manoeuvre before dragging the drunk to a standing position.

But that did nothing.

So, Constable Loxley bent down, to see...

...*something wet* near the body glistening, catching the light from the torch.

Loxley's stomach tightened. He reached down to hook the man's arm, to turn him around, so he could see up close what glistened all around him, like a thick muddy pool.

Something that Loxley had never seen in such quantity, and perhaps never expected to see in the town of Mydworth.

Blood.

So much of it.

For a second, Loxley wasn't sure what to do. Then he turned the body *over* so he could see the face and – more importantly – the wound.

There was no chance that the man would still be alive.

With so much blood lost, *that* would be clearly impossible.

But now, in the dim light from his torch, he saw two things.

The wound. Or actually, *wounds*, centred in the man's mid-section.

Whoever had done this had acted quickly, brutally. The sight of those wounds, intimidating, even – the Constable had to admit – frightening.

And then he noticed the other thing.

The man's face.

He recognised it.

It was the face of one of the men from the pub quarrel.

From the fight that Loxley had interrupted, and – he had thought – extinguished.

One of those men now dead.

He stood up, and stepped back from the body, as he ran through what needed to be done now.

His training – so recently completed – coming instinctively into play. Discovery of suspicious death, constable's priorities, list in order…

The body to be cordoned off, Sergeant Timms to be alerted. The alleyway to be sealed at both ends, examined minutely for evidence.

Loxley ticked off all the steps that would have to be taken.

The locals would soon become aware of the activity, torches, car lights. More police would need to be summoned from Chichester to assist.

Did the man have family? They would need to be awakened in the middle of the night, once the constabulary could answer the basic question of – *who was he?*

With the larger question pushed aside for now: *who wanted to kill this man… and why?*

Loxley gave himself a moment, a deep breath, the air chasing away the metallic smell that had filled his nostrils when he first bent down.

And before he started to do all that must be done, another thought came to him.

Perhaps sleepy Mydworth isn't so sleepy at all.

2.

MABEL'S LAST HOPE

HARRY RACED UP the steps of the Town Hall, snow flying from his warm camel trench coat. He wondered how Kat – who'd driven here earlier, all the way from Arundel – had fared with the Alvis in the snow.

Over breakfast she had laughed as the first flakes had fallen. "You call that *snow*? You should see what a winter Nor'easter looks like in January in New York. Back where I come from, Sir Harry, we'd label that a 'dusting'."

He had smiled. He did enjoy the way Kat gave his British view of things such a nice American twist. *Refreshing!*

Entering the hall, he saw groups of people busy decorating it – some on ladders hanging pink streamers, a few busily attaching large red crepe-paper hearts to the wall.

Winter might have thrown some weather at them, but in here? Spring looked ready to be sprung.

And then he saw Kat, with Aunt Lavinia. His wife was at the top of a ladder, stretching up to tack a twisted garland proclaiming "Happy Valentine's Day!" onto the centuries-old walls of the Town Hall.

Harry tossed his coat onto a folding chair, hurrying to Kat, whose fingertips appeared to be just a few inches shy of their target.

"The troops have arrived," he said, one hand out to steady the ladder.

Kat turned, ever stunning, even with what looked like her gardening trousers and a grey puffy fisherman's sweater, hair pulled back. *Amazing how she can pull off that look*, he thought, as she said: "Well, your aunt and I are in the market for gentlemen with a bit more of a, shall we say, reach?"

"Knew I was good for something."

And he watched as Kat came down the ladder and handed him the pink and white garland.

When he reached the top step of the ladder, he turned to both his Aunt Lavinia and Kat, saying, "I imagine I cut quite a figure like this, eh?"

"You remember what traditionally comes after pride, Harry?" said Kat, teasingly wobbling the ladder.

"Hey, steady now," said Harry. "Don't want to damage your Charleston partner for Saturday!"

KAT WAS LAUGHING at a story Lavinia told about last year's Valentine's Ball – something to do with a man in a tux that no longer came even close to fitting him – when she heard the doors to the hall swing open with a *bang*.

She turned to see Nicola, who ran the Women's Voluntary Service, and alongside her another woman, young, pretty, walking hand in hand with a little girl who clutched a stuffed bear tight.

Kat worked a couple of days a week for Nicola at the WVS, helping out with legal work and administration: the threadbare charity – such a good cause – supporting

Mydworth women with all kinds of problems, no questions asked.

Kat had mentioned to her yesterday that she was helping decorate the Town Hall for Saturday's charity ball – she guessed that Nicola was here to see her.

Kat watched them hurry over – the woman's eyes showing the marks of someone who had recently been crying.

Or – more to the point – *someone who had been crying a lot.*

Harry had turned away from his aunt, and now came beside Kat.

"What do we have here?" he said, as Nicola closed the distance, the speed and franticness of her arrival an odd contrast to the colourful garlands and crepe-paper hearts that decorated the hall.

Whatever lay ahead – it was clearly not festive.

AS WAS NICOLA'S style, she got quickly to the point.

"Kat, Sir Harry," then to Lavinia, "m'lady."

Kat saw Nicola pause to look at the obviously distressed woman beside her. "I wonder, if we could have a word in private? This is Mabel Brown. And little Elsie. It's about something rather serious."

Kat was nodding even before she reached the end of her sentence. Meanwhile, Lavinia, quick to act, took a step forward, and bent down to the towheaded little girl. "You *know*, I am sure I spied a plate of biscuits somewhere around here." Kat saw Lavinia shoot a look at the mother and Nicola. "Why don't you and I see if we can find them?"

The little girl, one hand holding her well-loved bear, the other her mother's hand, looked up at her mother, who was quick to nod.

Then Lavinia, the girl's hand now held gently in hers, said to Kat: "There's a small room you can use behind the stage. Nice and private."

And with that, as if taking little Elsie on some great adventure, Lavinia walked away with her, elaborating on the array of biscuits that awaited them.

"Shall we?" Kat said, indicating the side door that led to the back-stage area.

THEY PULLED FOUR chairs together to make a circle in a room filled with boxes of ancient props and decorations. Kat wished they had some tea at the ready.

At moments like this, she had learned, the stuff was positively essential.

Harry, she saw, kept an easy manner, projecting steadiness and reassuring calm.

"So, what seems to be the problem," he said, looking at Kat, then adding the vital words, "and how can we help?"

Nicola turned to Mabel whose hands were intertwined as if wrestling with each other over some dispute.

Kat thought she saw a glimmer of yet more tears in the corner of each eye.

"It's my Ollie," said Mabel, tentatively. "My husband."

The woman took the deepest of breaths.

"Y-you see – he's in Pentonville Prison in London. And they're going to hang him! Friday at dawn. Dawn!"

And with those rather amazing words, the young woman fell apart, sobbing, heaving as Nicola draped an arm around her.

While all waited for this terrible storm – if not to end – to at least subside.

HARRY HANDED THE woman his folded handkerchief, and she wiped her eyes, then began to talk again.

"They said he killed Ben Carmody. *Murdered* him."

Harry took his seat. He knew the case. Wasn't often that Mydworth was rocked by such a grisly affair. The young chap, Carmody, had been found brutally stabbed in a narrow cut-through on the edge of the town, just up from Hill Lane.

The evidence, as reported in the *Mydworth Mercury,* overwhelming: a bloody knife found at the house of Oliver Brown; as well as a shirt – dappled in blood – discovered in his vegetable patch. Buried, but apparently too quickly, and easily found.

He and Kat had talked about the case when the lurid details first came out, following developments through the courts to the final guilty verdict before Christmas at the Old Bailey in London.

With Kat's background working for a New York criminal lawyer, she had agreed: there seemed little doubt that Oliver Brown had murdered his old friend in a drunken rage.

In desperation, it seemed, the defence had resorted to pleading that the whole affair should be seen as a crime of passion; there'd been absolutely no attempt to deny that Brown had struck the fatal blows.

For now, Harry held back any questions – the most important of which would be, *What on earth could he and Kat do to help this woman and her husband? Justice had reached its decision.*

At one point, Nicola added details: "The WVS were able to arrange a solicitor to manage the case. Charles Strudwick… you know him?"

Harry nodded. Strudwick was an elderly and perfectly adequate partner in one of Mydworth's oldest practices. Eminently respectable, but perhaps not someone you'd want to entrust with your life in a murder trial.

"Anyway, Mr Strudwick's barrister in London won an appeal last month. Hoping for more information to come to light."

Harry thought, *With all the evidence as reported in the paper, what more information could possibly be needed?*

"The lawyers did the best they could, I'm sure," Nicola said, "but we just heard this morning, the appeal failed."

"And my Ollie didn't do it!" Mabel said.

Of course, Harry thought, *that's what any wife would claim about their accused husband.*

He saw Kat lean forward, reach out and take Mabel's two hands in hers. Hold them. Then very gently she said, "Can you tell us, why you think that, Mabel? Why you believe your husband isn't guilty?"

And Harry saw that Kat's grasp – gentle and supportive – had given the woman some strength to tell what she believed.

Now it would be a simple question: would her words be anything that *they too* could believe?

3.

BEN AND OLLIE

"MY OLLIE WOULDN'T kill anyone," said Mabel, as if the very notion was patently obvious. "I mean, he has a temper all right, and he can get into a spot of trouble. But kill someone? Never!"

Harry glanced at Kat. *Was this the defence? It didn't stand for much.*

"I read in the reports," Kat said, "that Ben and your husband were old friends?"

"Yes. I mean, they knew each other – all grew up in Mydworth, didn't we? Course, Ben had come up in the world, and my Ollie, still, well, just a farmhand. But they were never enemies, not really."

Harry found the choice of the words *"not really"* rather interesting.

So did Kat, apparently.

"But there had been – or was – *something?*"

Yes, Harry thought, *she sensed something* not *being said here.*

Least, not yet.

Mabel looked again to Nicola as if she needed a bit of a prod to say what she was about to say. Then, "Long time ago, we three all knew each other, and, and… well, Ben and me, we was going together then. Ollie used to joke that Ben still carried a torch for me. But I told him, time moves on, Ollie."

She paused.

"But there *was* that… history, yes."

"And what about the night it all happened?" Kat said. "Did you see Ollie when he came home from the pub?"

"No. I'd gone to bed, hadn't I?"

Harry glanced at Kat again, now remembering the woman's testimony as written in the papers.

"So, you don't actually know what time he got in?" said Harry.

"Well, it was later. After the pub closed. That's what I said in court."

Harry smiled and nodded at that. "But – you can't be sure?"

Mabel shrugged away the obvious point.

"He woke me up with his snoring. Asleep on the rocker, by the fire, he was. Always snored, he did, after a few pints."

"So nothing unusual about that night?" said Kat.

"No. Only the police coming round at dawn, banging on the door, taking my Ollie away…"

Harry could see that Mabel was about to break down again, but Kat put a hand on her shoulder. "That must have been so frightening."

"It *was*. And little Elsie, she didn't understand."

Harry watched how gently Kat asked questions.

"They had been at the Station Inn?" she said. "Lot of drinks I guess?"

Mabel nodded. "My Ollie, he liked his ale. Could get a bit out of order. But never nasty with it, you know? Not like a lot of the lads."

"But there had been a bit of a fight, hadn't there, earlier in the evening?" Harry asked, doing his best to be as gentle as his wife had been.

Mabel hesitated, then said slowly, "The police was called. Seems the two of them got into some kind of dustup. But no real harm done. Things all calmed down, with Will there."

Will. Not a name Harry remembered from the newspaper story.

"Will?" he asked.

Mabel nodded. "Will Davis. One of the lads, he is. Was with them in the pub. All friends together, see? Whatever happened, had passed."

Then Mabel began shaking her head. "My Ollie has a temper, yes. But he loves me – loves our little Elsie – more than anything in the world. He wouldn't—" the words hard now, with lips quivering "—get angry and throw it all away."

And she looked up, through what were now constantly glistening pools.

"It's only three days away. Three days, and I lose my husband; my little girl her father. Please, m'lady, Sir Harry… help me."

Harry was ready to answer but Kat beat him to the punch.

"Mabel, I'm not sure what Sir Harry and I can do. But I guess Nicola has all the details?"

Mabel nodded, the slim offer of hope having its affect.

Kat turned to Harry. "We can look into things. See if anything was missed from the evidence."

Mabel leaned out of her chair and – like grasping a lone rocky outcrop in a raging sea – gave Kat the biggest hug.

At which point Harry heard his aunt enter, chattering away with her new charge.

"Ah, *there's* your mother. Elsie here was wondering where you were." Lavinia leaned down to the little girl, still holding half a biscuit. "Though we had the *grandest* time – with our oatmeal biscuits – looking at all the decorations."

The little girl went to her mother, who stood up.

Kat looked at Mabel. "We'll do our best. But please don't think we can promise anything."

"But you'll *try*?" Mabel said.

Harry answered that one. "We will absolutely do *that*."

And then, feeling that they were now facing an impossible task, he watched as Nicola, with a grateful smile to Kat, escorted the woman and her little girl from the stock room, and out to the hall.

It was Lavinia who pointed out the obvious.

"I know the case. From the papers, of course. You two have your work cut out for you."

To which Kat replied, "Do we ever…"

KAT PUSHED OPEN the heavy door of the Town Hall and pulled her coat tight against the falling snow.

"How about we leave the Alvis here, walk back to the Dower House?" said Harry, as he joined her. "I can pop down, pick it up later."

"Good idea," said Kat. "I take back what I said about New York. This English snow? Looking like the real thing. Quite beautiful, actually."

She took Harry's arm, and together they plodded across the square and up the High Street, the snow shin-deep.

THE WRONG MAN

Around them, in the gathering darkness, she saw the shops all shutting early, the gas lights in the street already lit, throwing pools of yellow light.

A bunch of delighted kids on the corner were throwing snowballs.

"Harry," she said, snuggling against his warm coat as they walked. "The evidence does sound damning."

"To say the least. The murder weapon found. The bloody shirt. And what happened at the pub beforehand?"

"I just couldn't bear to say 'no' to her."

"Oh, me too. You know, Kat, I do understand how the people in the lovely town of Mydworth have come to appreciate our rather unlikely skills. But rabbits out of hats? Tough call, as your fellow New Yorkers would say."

"Agree. Totally."

She held his arm tight, the thought of Mabel's husband facing the gallows... such a grim image.

Especially leaving behind that little girl.

"I have an idea. You're in London tomorrow, aren't you?" she said.

"Don't remind me. Another interminable meeting, yes," said Harry. "Early train – if it's still running."

"Then home for the rest of the week?"

"That's the general idea."

"So, we're not too busy, are we?"

"Not terribly," said Harry.

They walked in silence for another minute, treading carefully in the thick snow. Then, at the crossroads by the Green Man, she turned to him, their breath making small clouds in the chilly evening air.

"It's just... I wondered... what with you being at the Foreign Office and all, maybe you could pull some

18

strings in London? You *must* know someone who *knows someone?*"

"Not sure that my knowing *anyone* can stop the wheels of justice and the dire fate ahead for Oliver Brown."

Kat nodded at that.

"Not even to win a delay? Another appeal? Worth pursuing, right? I mean, really?"

Harry nodded, but then looked away as if there was something troubling him.

"Trouble is, it all comes back to the small matter of the damned – and damning – evidence," he said. "All pointing in the direction of Oliver Brown having stabbed Ben Carmody."

"I know. But can I let you in on a little secret?"

"Why do I think I'm about to hear a tale from the great metropolis of Manhattan?"

She laughed, as they stood now for a moment at the foot of their drive. "Because you *are*. My work for that defence attorney? Know what we saw, more than just a few times? Evidence that seemed magically to 'pop' up. The police, the DA—"

"Sorry, DA?"

"District Attorney. The city's prosecutor. Both eager to close a case, get their suspect in jail, and move onto other things."

"While the real killer goes free?"

"Exactly. So, listen, Harry," she grabbed his forearm, "why don't we, in the days ahead, talk to anyone connected to the two men? *Look* for another motive. Another suspect. Look for any secrets. Anything – and everything. Worth a shot don't you think?"

Harry fixed his eyes on her. *He's thinking this over*, Kat thought.

"Not terribly sure at this point. But," Harry took her arm again as they headed up the drive towards the house, "well – dammit – why not?" he said turning to her. "The hangman, as they say, waits for no man."

And with the sudden idea – the *possibility*, even though she had not a jot of proof – that there could have been a mistake in the judgement, Kat took a deep breath.

Then, as if simply planning another festive activity to accompany the upcoming weekend's charity ball, she said: "Shall we plot and plan? Now, I mean. Right now?"

"Absolutely. Quick cup of tea, warm up by the fire, then carry on over dinner?"

"Of course. Wouldn't think about starting an adventure like this without the mandatory pot of tea!"

And Harry laughed, as they stepped up to the porch of the Dower House, the air cold, crisp, and the snow crunching below their feet.

4.

THE CASE BEGINS

"Thank you, Maggie," Harry said as their housekeeper put down the tray with two plates of bacon, eggs, mushrooms and tomatoes.

The sunroom at the side of the house, small but perfectly comfortable, was catching the first glimmerings of the rising sun. A winter sun, but still – through the glass – not without warmth.

"Yours is the runny egg, sir, just as you like it," said Maggie. "Top up the teapot, shall I?"

"Maggie, you are a godsend," said Harry, buttering toast as Maggie took the teapot away to refill it.

"You don't have to butter me up to get a spot more tea, Harry," she said over her shoulder as she left the room.

He laughed at that.

Maggie had been by his side for so long. More than a housekeeper, that's for sure.

Harry leaned over to his wife. "Whatever would we do without her?"

"Eat less, that's for sure. I mean, we both know the extent of your cooking skills—"

"Hey there – no need to be harsh, now. Think I successfully scrambled an egg once."

"Scrambled?" said Kat. "*Confused* it, more like."

Kat, grinning, took a mouthful of toast; a scattering of crumbs on her lower lip. Harry knew they had important things to do now, not least the coming rush to the station.

Still, looking at her now, bathed in that morning sunlight?

Well, one could be excused for thoughts of procrastination.

"All right – back to the plan, then," he said. "Think we're sorted? I bow to your expertise."

Kat nodded. "Well, I didn't run real investigations in New York. Took depositions, sure. Spoke to people. But I did get rather involved in an incident or two in my postings."

"The Istanbul affair? Sounded a tad dangerous when you told me about *that* one."

"More than a *tad*, dear Harry. But okay, start at the beginning with the victim. I've got an address for Ben Carmody. Lodgings out on a place called Blackmead Farm. You know it?"

"Rings a bell," said Harry. "Up off the Arundel Road, I think? Good luck in this snow. What then?"

"The crime scene, for sure – and the victim."

"Absolutely. Still thinking of another chat with the wife, too?"

"Probably," said Kat. "But that – maybe later. I want to talk to the constable who discovered the body first."

"Relatively new to the post, I remember from the newspaper reports."

They waited while Maggie reappeared with the teapot, then returned to the kitchen.

"What about the solicitor?" said Kat. "You know him?"

"Decent enough chap. Not sure he'll be much help. But it would be good form to let him know we're taking a look at the case. I might have an angle   on the barrister in London."

Another bite of toast, and the crumb disappeared.

"You keeping an eye on the time?" said Kat.

"Oops," said Harry. "Breakfast – and the company – too delicious to leave."

Kat laughed at that. "Don't you worry. I'll give you a lift, check out Ben's lodgings, then on to the police station."

"Enjoy your encounter with Sergeant Timms."

"*Encounter*? Is that what you'd call it?"

"Hardly the face of modern policing, now is he? Okay, that's your day planned. Here's hoping I can somehow get access to Pentonville."

"That poor man," said Kat. "A noose only days away."

"Yes. But remember, that poor man – until we know otherwise – is still a brutal killer."

"Think you do a very good job of reminding me, Harry."

"I imagine it's why you love me," he said, getting up and giving her a kiss, then putting on his jacket. He grinned. "It is, isn't it?"

Kat laughed, and then she quickly drained her tea cup, standing as well.

"Oh. Let's not forget. There's the third man to track down," Kat said.

"The *who*?"

"Will Davis – the peacemaker Mabel mentioned? Think we can meet him together?"

"Good idea."

And with that, Harry grabbed his coat and briefcase. Maggie had informed them that a roast chicken would be waiting for them for dinner: roast potatoes, her secret raisin stuffing, and her special carrots that tasted more like dessert than the obligatory vegetable.

At which point, thought Harry, *we might just know if all this fuss is a waste of time – Oliver Brown's fate sealed.*

Or maybe *not.*

And as Harry opened the front door, he said: "I do love all this domesticity. You know, breakfasts, roast dinners, wife running me to the station…"

"But much *more* fun with our little extracurriculars?"

"Birds of a feather."

And they left the cosy Dower House. Already Harry could see the morning growing chillier again, blue skies now dotted with looming grey clouds.

Maybe even more snow on the way.

KAT DROPPED HARRY off at the station, barely in time for him to race up the platform stairs to catch the 8.14 to London Victoria, then coaxed the Alvis back through the snowy streets and out onto the Arundel Road.

From there she took at least two wrong turns before she finally spotted a tilted, sad-looking sign announcing "Blackmead Farm" – just a dirt road with deep, snow-filled ruts, giving the Alvis a steady stream of nasty shakes as it rumbled up to the house.

And the house…?

As a girl, Kat had a time where she enjoyed reading scary books, especially late at night, with a Hudson Valley thunderstorm roaring outside, sending lightning streaking across the summer sky.

She'd be curled up with Mary Shelley's *Frankenstein*, or – even more amazing, more terrifying – Bram Stoker's *Dracula*.

And often, when done reading – or strongly urged to go to bed by her father – she used to wish that maybe her room light could *stay* on.

Now, seeing this house here, she was reminded of those books. Probably quite grand in its day, the farmhouse now looked ominous; signs of neglect and decay everywhere.

Paint visibly peeling – and any paint that remained, faded to the dullest of browns. The front garden – if that was what it was – even though covered in snow, showed the signs of being let go; odd clumps of ragged vegetation shrugging through the white.

Not the cheeriest place for Ben Carmody to live, she thought.

She slowed the car, pulling it close to the front door. No sign of any other vehicles and – at first – no sign of anyone living here at all.

Kat wondered if she might possibly have the wrong place. The house looked completely abandoned.

There was only one way to find out.

SHE STOOD ON the top step and rapped on the door, its splintery wood in dire need of repair.

No answer. She knocked again, hearing the sound echoing through the eerie old house.

She was about to give up when the door opened, creaking on rusty hinges.

A woman stood there, the same age as Kat – give or take – wearing the demure and drab costume of a housekeeper.

Her hair pulled back. No makeup that Kat could see. The dress, a pale grey, falling to the mid-calf, and with severe black shoes that matched the role and look.

"*Yes*? Can I help you?"

Kat smiled, and hoped this surprise visit didn't bring about a quick rejection of her request.

"Yes. Hi. I'm Lady Mortimer—" thinking that might help "—and I was hoping I could have a word with the owner of the house?"

"Can I ask what it's about?" said the woman, eyeing Kat suspiciously.

"It's to do with Ben Carmody."

The woman didn't allow her face to register anything.

"Ben Carmody is *dead*. Has been for some months now."

Kat nodded as if what the woman said made perfect sense.

"I know," she said. "I need to talk to the owner of the house. Is he at home?"

"Mr Urquhart's *always* at home."

Kat waited, the woman still peering intently at her around the half-open door, fresh flakes of snow now beginning to swirl about them both. Then, finally, Kat saw the woman hold the door open wider.

"You'd better come in."

Kat did as she was told, stepping into a dark hallway, the interior barely any warmer than the outside.

She took in the place: bare stone-tiled floor, dark wallpaper peeling from the walls, brown-painted doors firmly shut, a corridor leading to the rear of the house where, Kat sensed, perhaps a warmer kitchen lay.

"I'm Connie Price, the housekeeper," said the woman, pushing the door shut and turning to her. "Mr Urquhart's up in his rooms, but – I must warn you – speaking to him can be quite a challenge."

Kat kept smiling, adding quickly, "I do like challenges. And thank you."

26

"This way then," said the housekeeper, cutting her short.

Kat followed her across the hall to a flight of stairs.

Those stairs, covered by the darkest maroon carpets, were wide enough to support a parade of family traipsing down, perhaps to see what good old Santa had left under the tree. Kat had the feeling this grim place maybe didn't host so many festive events any more.

She noted that the place had electricity, but it wasn't being put to an extensive use. A single lamp with tassels lit the staircase.

Connie walked steadily ahead of her, and as they reached the top of the stairs and turned to go down a long, dark corridor past more brown-painted doors, Kat heard a muffled voice ahead of them.

"Who's there?" came the voice, plaintive, strained. "I hear you! Who is it? Connie? Is it you?"

The housekeeper stopped at the end of the corridor, and opened the last door to reveal a sitting room, lit only by another dim floor lamp in the corner.

"Mr Urquhart," said Connie, stepping into the room while Kat paused behind her in the doorway.

Most of the furniture in the room was covered with once-white cloths, all now turned dingy. Just a table and an old desk, scattered with papers, stood uncovered.

On the floor was another thick carpet – ancient, colours faded – with sprawling swirls that looked either like dragons or exotic plants.

A door at the far end of the room stood open. Through it, Kat could see a single bed, and next to it a washbowl and a table crammed with bottles of ointments, medications.

The paraphernalia that goes with caring for the elderly, the same the world over — so familiar from her own father's last years.

Back in the sitting room, caught in the flickering light from a spluttering fire, Kat saw the old man himself, propped up in a wing chair, wrapped in a faded blanket, a tattered, quilted hat on his head like a Victorian gentleman.

Kat watched him slowly peer round the side of the armchair and croak at the housekeeper: "Connie! It *is* you! Wherever have you been? I heard voices! Can't you hear them as—"

Then the man noticed Kat standing in the doorway.

"Who's that? There! In the darkness! Step forward. Show yourself!"

Kat walked into the room, wondering...

Could this timid old man somehow help her uncover a hidden truth about Ben Carmody's death?

Or was she just wasting time?

The hours to the hanging, ticking away.

5.

BEN CARMODY

MR URQUHART TOOK out a pair of glasses from the top pocket of his dressing gown, wiped them on his sleeve, put them on and peered at Kat.

"All right then. Who exactly are *you*?"

Kat thought, *The old man's faculties wobbly, and his eyesight clearly none too good.*

She took some steps forward, and stretched out her hand.

Urquhart might be over 80 years old, but Kat saw the faint flicker of a spark in his eyes as if picking up a glow from the coals in the fire. Frail or not – he still maybe had some of his wits about him.

"This is Lady Mortimer," said Connie.

"*Lady* Mortimer eh? You can't be here soliciting for war bonds, yes? All that nonsense is over. So, m'lady…"

"Mr Urquhart—"

"*Jeremiah*, please!"

Kat smiled, encouraged by his unexpected liveliness. "I was hoping to—"

"And *Lady* Mortimer – an *American*, to boot? Didn't even know my country allowed such things. I went to America once you know! Texas!"

"It's a beautiful state," said Kat.

"Towns are nice. But that countryside? Just desert and oil far as the eye can see. And tumbleweeds everywhere!"

"Did you live there?" said Kat, smiling at the old man's strange recollections.

"Good Lord no. Are you mad, Lady Mortimer? Too hot! Far too hot! Didn't stay long. Came home soon as I could." He leaned close to Kat. "Now sit, sit! We can have a nice chat. Connie fetch us a pot of tea. Cups too."

Kat saw the old man grin at his own witticism.

She looked around for an uncovered chair, finally seeing a straight-backed chair, the wood covered in peeling gilt, the seat a tattered red brocade.

It would do just fine as she told *Jeremiah* exactly why she was here – if he would give her the chance.

"I *SEE*," the old man said when Kat finally was able to explain what she was looking into. And amazingly enough, after all this time, she saw two small wet pools in the corner of the man's eyes.

"Loved that lad, I did. Like he was my own son."

Kat saw him look up now to the mantelpiece – to a framed photo of a man in officer's uniform.

"That's my own brave boy, Arthur," said Jeremiah. "Lost him in '16. So, after the war, I needed help running the farm – some of the village lads came to work for me. Ben was the best, though. But then, he moved on. Made something of himself, you know?"

Kat took a sip of the tea. She noticed her cup had the smallest of chips, though she was sure that an inspection of its underside would reveal that it was once a very fine and pricey cup.

"That is why, when he came back to Mydworth, it made me *so* glad."

Kat nodded as the man talked. He dabbed at his eyes. "And what happened to him… terrible. I just don't even know what to—"

Kat put up a hand, gently, simply signalling that the two of them didn't have to go into *all that*.

Instead, she had another question.

"He lived here for a while, yes?"

"Well, even when he moved away, he always used to pop back to visit every now and then. Checking up on me, he said. And then he came home to the village, got himself a proper job – a good job – was looking for a place to stay, just a room, he said. Well—" Urquhart laughed. "Got plenty of *those* here. He insisted I take the rent money. Think he knew how *difficult* things were. Helped me pay dear Connie. She's such a good sort too, you know. Ha! Just to put up with me, Lady Mortimer."

Another conspiratorial lean forward towards Kat.

"And *that* is no easy task. But I'll see her right. When I'm gone. She deserves it."

Kat nodded, but from the dire state of the house, she couldn't imagine there would be more than pennies to leave to the young housekeeper.

The house… probably worth less than the old man's debts.

She waited while he stared into the flames.

"We all go, in the end, don't we?" he said. "But I have nothing to complain about. So many are taken too early."

Kat nodded. "You miss Ben."

Another long pause and, despite his irascible nature, the man's face fell. "I do. I do indeed."

Then he turned back to her, his voice suddenly brighter.

"Sometimes, you know, I think I hear him. Still here, in the house! Wandering about downstairs. Talking. Laughing. Must be imagining things."

"Really?" said Kat, trying not to sound disbelieving, and saddened at Jeremiah's confusion. "Old place like this, must creak and groan a bit."

"Yes. Right. That's what Connie says. But – here's the thing – I'm not 'mad'. I know what I hear. *Saw* him too one night, with my own eyes, in this very room."

Kat just nodded. There was no doubt he believed what he had seen.

As the man spoke, he became more agitated. Then he reached out and touched Kat's hand.

"Listen to this. I was in bed. I heard a noise out here. It was so dark, but, in the firelight, there he was! By the desk. Right... right there! Clear as day! I called out to him – Ben! I said, Ben my boy! – but he turned away, hurried downstairs, too quick for me. I was going to follow – but the stairs, ha! Connie says I mustn't use them. Doctor too. My *condition* they call it. Bah, condition! Just because I've tripped up a couple of times."

Kat could imagine the young housekeeper having trouble looking after this old gentleman.

She decided not pursue any questions about the sighting of Ben's ghost.

"Jeremiah, did Ben ever have any enemies?"

"Enemies? That boy? Never! Everybody *loved* Ben. Good old Ben, they'd say. Generous to a 't', steady and dependable as they come!"

Kat smiled.

"Yes. That's what I've heard too," she said. Then, seeing the old man slump back in his chair she quickly added: "Wondering… do you think I could look at his chambers?"

"His room? Just along the corridor there. Nothing's been moved. I told Connie – leave it just the way it is."

Kat smiled and leaned forward to pat the man's right hand. There was something special about that hand, looking like something painted by Rembrandt.

Aged, fragile, and yet, Kat thought, precious. Even beautiful.

Then the man turned, and shouted as best he could: "Connie!"

CONNIE PUSHED OPEN the door to the room at the far end of the long dreary hallway. Again, it was lit by a single lamp, the shade stained yellow, struggling to provide some way to light the path.

But Ben Carmody's room had a window facing south, and – with the sun rising higher – that sun had filled the small room, making it seem almost cheery. Out of the window, Kat could just see the distant buildings of Mydworth, the tall church steeple.

And laid out in front of them, snow-covered fields, probably once home to herds of cattle and sheep.

Those days clearly long gone.

She also thought: *How will Urquhart be able to stay on, afford Connie, with Ben's rent gone?*

"Do you mind me asking, m'lady, what you got to do with Ben?" said the housekeeper, still standing in the room behind her.

Kat turned.

"My husband, Sir Harry Mortimer and I are looking into the case, for a friend, you see. Put them at ease that nothing was missed."

And this seemed to spark something in the dour woman before her.

"Missed? What do you mean – *missed?*"

Interesting reaction, that word hitting a nerve.

But why?

"Yes. You know how people think. Worried that, somehow, they didn't get all the facts. So yes—"

Again...

"—*missed.*"

The woman nodded, but stayed, hovering, as Kat looked around the room.

"His things?" Kat asked.

"There wasn't much. Some clothes. A book he was reading. Notebooks related to his work in the electrical shop. Packed it all up and sent it to his next of kin, some cousin in Manchester."

"Ah," said Kat, sliding open an empty drawer – then another.

Apart from a crucifix above the bed, and a faded print of Brighton seafront, nothing remained in this room of Ben Carmody.

It was as if the place had been... *scoured.*

Strange...

"Mr Urquhart told me that nothing in here had been touched," said Kat, opening a small wardrobe bare even of hangars.

"He forgets things. Gets them wrong. I told him what I had done."

34

Kat nodded. "No other family?"

She had a feeling that she had to *press* Connie. The woman was – for some reason – reluctant. But why?

"Lost his dad in the Great War. His mum, well, she couldn't go on without him. Jeremiah took him under his wing. Gave him work, sure. Was like a dad to him as well."

So – Jeremiah lost his own son, and then this young orphan had turned up on the farm to help out. No wonder the two had a special bond.

Kat paused. The next question, a difficult one.

"Connie, can you think of any reason someone would have wanted Ben Carmody dead?"

"But Oliver Brown did it, didn't he? They convicted him – so he did it, right?"

Bit of an edge there, thought Kat. *She's acting like she's got something to hide.*

Kat looked around the spartan room. The narrow bed, the simple chest of drawers.

"Everybody liked Ben," said Connie.

"No enemies, then? That you know of?"

"I said 'no', Lady Mortimer."

Kat smiled. "That you did. Just wondering if maybe something came to mind. Some encounter?"

"Ben Carmody had no enemies."

If there was one thing Kat knew, it was that anyone, anywhere, might have an enemy.

So why was Connie so confident?

"Can I ask you one more question?" Kat said. Connie stood there, and without giving her assent, waited. "Mr Urquhart… will he be able to get on? I mean with Ben and that rent gone?"

THE WRONG MAN

"Long enough," said Connie. "The doctor told me that he hasn't got long. Every day could be his last."

"He doesn't know?"

"Suspects maybe. But that's it."

"He talked about his… condition?"

"Makes him wobbly," said Connie. "Confused. Tired. Imagines things, as you see. What's ahead for him is maybe for the best – know what I mean?"

Kat wondered how the old man's passing would affect this woman?

She *seemed* to have affection for Urquhart. But, without the financial support, how long could she hang on here, working?

Kat took one last moment to look in the woman's eyes.

Funny thing about secrets, she thought.

Try as you might, somehow there is always that tell-tale sign of something not *being said. Not being revealed.*

And that secret?

Time to dig deeper, she thought.

"Have you worked here long, Connie?" said Kat, softening her tone.

"Since school," said Connie, with a shrug, as if there had never been any other options for her.

"And you and Ben were here for years together?" said Kat. "Were you close?"

"Like family, we were."

"Must have been a busy farm, back in the day?"

No answer, though Kat felt she saw in the woman's eyes, perhaps some longing for those times.

"And now… just you and Mr Urquhart? Not easy, hmm?"

"It's what I do, m'lady. I'm happy with my own company. And taking care of the dear man."

"I'm sure Mr Urquhart is   very grateful."

"I can't complain."

Kat could sense Connie wanting to close this conversation. *Time to change tack.*

"That night – the night Ben died – do you remember much about what happened?"

But before the young housekeeper could answer, Kat heard Urquhart calling from his room, his voice panicky.

"Connie! Connie! I can't find my *tea*!"

"I'd better go," said Connie.

"Don't worry," said Kat. "I understand. I can see myself out."

As Connie turned and headed down the corridor to deal with Jeremiah, his voice still clamouring, Kat toyed with the idea of maybe sneaking a look around downstairs.

But then decided; *Better to come back again, maybe with Harry. There were more questions to ask.*

Especially now with her every instinct telling her that Connie was hiding something. But what?

Was it connected to Ben Carmody? Well, time – Kat hoped – would tell.

That is – if there was enough time.

6.

AN OPEN-AND-SHUT CASE

KAT DROVE CAREFULLY back into town, the streets still
quiet, snow banked high in the hedgerows. She parked outside
Mydworth Police Station.

The steps up to the front door had been swept and salted,
but were still dotted with treacherous icy patches.

Inside, as she pushed open the door and entered, she saw
the portly figure of Sergeant Timms at the desk, pipe in one
hand, mug in the other, and a newspaper open in front of him.

Hard at work fighting crime!

A compact fire blazed in the hearth.

"Aha, um, Lady Mortimer!" said Timms, hurriedly
pushing the paper to one side, standing and dragging a ledger
across in its place.

"Sergeant Timms, good morning."

"How may I be of assistance, m'lady?" said the police
sergeant, slipping round the desk and pulling out a chair for
Kat to sit in.

As he retreated to his side of the desk, Kat saw a couple of
faces peer out at her from the back office, then retreat out of
sight.

Timms' two constables, she guessed. *One of them perhaps the chap
who'd found the body?*

"Brisk morning," said Timms. "A cup of tea, perhaps?"

"Kind of you, sergeant, but I'm not stopping," said Kat, sitting and unbuttoning her coat in the warm room. "I have a favour to ask."

"Oh yes?" said Timms. "Anything at all that the Mydworth Police can do to assist, m'lady." Though – from Timms' grumbling tone – it sounded to Kat more like "*oh dear*".

The sergeant's patience with Kat and Harry's little investigations – which certainly didn't show him or the department in a competent light – had grown *thin* in recent months, she knew.

"You will have heard that Oliver Brown's appeal has been dismissed?" she said.

"Yes, m'lady. Good thing, too," said Timms. "Waste of everybody's time, that was."

"Wheels of justice," said Kat, with what she hoped was a sympathetic shrug.

"Ah yes, though those wheels do come off sometimes, don't they?"

"Indeed they do," said Kat, knowing that she and Timms were now talking about two completely different things.

Which suddenly seemed to dawn on the sergeant.

"Er, you're surely not here to look into the Brown case," said Timms. "*Are* you?"

"Just a review, Sergeant Timms," said Kat. "For a friend. You know – dotting i's, crossing t's. Man's life in the balance, so to speak."

"Really," said Timms. "And, forgive me for asking, but what precisely does *that* mean?"

THE WRONG MAN

"Speaking to witnesses. Examining the scene of the crime. Talking to the constable who found the body, perhaps."

Kat watched as Timms did his best to put on his full-on disgruntled face.

"And on *whose* behalf are you doing this?"

"The WVS."

"Oh. I see. Brown's wife – poor lady – putting her *oar* in again, is she?"

Kat smiled. "Not terribly sure what that means. Oar? But I'd guess you'd agree that Mrs Brown certainly has a right to try and save her husband?"

"To the bitter end, it would seem," said Timms, his voice rising. "All rather useless, as I am sure you understand. Doesn't mean we all have to 'jump' when the woman says 'jump'."

"Of course not," said Kat calmly, refusing to respond in kind. "But we all want justice, do we not?"

"I dare say you wouldn't be questioning 'justice' if you'd seen the state of that poor lad Carmody. Trust me. In this case, justice *is* the hanging of Oliver Brown, and a hanging there shall be, I am glad to say."

Timms is in rare form this morning, thought Kat, smiling to herself. "So – to be clear, sergeant – we *can't* discuss this?"

She saw Timms slide the ledger closer and remove his pen from the inkwell.

"I'm afraid not," he said. "*Far* too busy, as you can see. And, as we say in this country – perhaps yours too – *case closed*!"

Kat nodded at that. This was proving challenging indeed.

"What about the constable who found the body? Bert Loxley, I believe? You think he might be able to give me five minutes?"

40

"The new lad? Oh, I don't think so," said Timms pointedly. "He's filing reports. Learning the ropes."

"Tomorrow perhaps?"

"I'm afraid *not*."

"Let me guess. More reports to file?"

"A policeman's lot, as the song goes."

Kat watched him, said nothing. She wondered if 'Sir Harry' were here, making the request, would *he* have gotten the same treatment? She doubted it.

She knew her crime in Timms' eyes.

Being a woman. Yes – then being American. And probably being an interfering pain in the—

"Lady Mortimer," he said, sitting back and folding his arms. "May I be frank?"

"Go ahead."

"*Nobody* wants this case opened up again. It was a nasty thing that happened, and now it's over. We all want to forget. Oliver Brown murdered Ben Carmody. He was tried and found guilty. And on Friday morning he will hang for it. End of story."

Kat remained motionless. Timms was not going to be persuaded. Time to move on. *The clock was ticking.*

She stood and buttoned her coat.

"Thank you for your candour, Sergeant Timms," she said. "Let's hope you're right."

Then she turned and left.

OUTSIDE, THE SKY was still grey – ominous and threatening – but it hadn't started snowing again.

THE WRONG MAN

The solicitor's office, had to be the next port of call, so she turned to head towards the square.

But she'd only gone a few yards before she heard a voice from behind her.

"Lady Mortimer."

She turned – to see one of the constables, hurrying from the side door of the police station, shrugging his coat on over his shoulders.

A quick look backwards over that shoulder as if checking to see if anyone might have spotted him.

"Sorry. I heard what you were saying to the sergeant," he said, coming close. "And I was thinking... maybe I can help?"

"Yes?" said Kat.

"Name's Loxley."

"Ah – you found the body?" said Kat.

"That's right."

She examined him more closely. Young, clean features. Determined looking.

"Can you tell me where that was?" she said.

"I can do more than that," he said. "I can *show* you."

"I wouldn't want you to get into trouble," said Kat, shooting a glance back at the station.

"Ha, don't worry about that," said Loxley, grinning. "Old Timms won't leave that chair until he's had at least two more cups of tea."

Kat laughed. Already she liked this young policeman. "All right then, constable – what are we waiting for?" said Kat.

And together they walked up the snowy road towards Hill Lane.

To the scene of the crime.

7.

SLIP-KNOT ALLEY

KAT WALKED WITH Loxley down Rosemary Lane, then back up Hill Lane towards the centre of the village. The town was eerily silent, the roads and sidewalks still thick with snow, but she saw that the clouds were now thinning: the sky above, a hazy blue.

She'd been in Mydworth a while now, and was beginning to know her way around its patchwork of lanes and roads – but she was surprised when the constable crossed the lane and gestured to a gap between a pair of cottages that was barely a couple of feet wide.

"It's called 'Slip-Knot Alley'," he said. "Gets a bit wider further up."

He turned and disappeared into the tiny alleyway. She passed through the gap too, and followed him, past hedges and tall brick walls until the alley took a final curve to the right, and emptied into an open area, the grass sleeping for winter, covered in white.

Loxley had stopped and was waiting for her. Behind him, across the field, she could see the rolling shape of the downs, snow-covered, dotted with trees.

The scene of the crime, Kat thought, *looking strangely magical.*

"Well, here we are," said the policeman, nodding towards a clump of snow-covered grass at the mouth of the alley. "The body was just to the side, there, curled up."

"No snow, I guess, back in November – so no helpful footprints?" said Kat, stepping back and taking in the scene.

"Exactly."

"This your first murder?" she said, watching the young man keenly.

"Won't be the last, I'm sure," he said with a shrug.

But Kat suspected he wasn't as casual about this as his tone implied.

"Can you talk me through what happened that night? The call to the pub? Where you met the victim, the murder suspect?"

Kat saw Loxley pause now, as if maybe having cold feet about getting involved.

"I'm not sure… It's all in the records, you can read it."

"I know. But sometimes going through it all again can bring back a memory, a feeling, maybe even a fact that just might be important."

"And might not?"

"Sure." She smiled. "But how about we try? I *have* done this before, you see."

That seemed to put the young policeman at ease.

"Okay," he said finally. "That night, back in November. I was on a late shift, so I had the night rounds. It was a cold evening, no rain…"

Kat listened carefully as he described his first routine tour of the town, then the phone call from the pub as he grabbed a quick cup of tea back at the station.

"When I got down there, well, it was pretty rowdy. Saturday night, see? And the Station Inn, well, it's not a pub

44

where you'd take your mother for a glass of sherry, if you know what I mean."

"I grew up in a bar in the Bronx, constable," said Kat. "Even worked in it. I know exactly what you mean."

She saw Loxley's eyebrows raise at that. She guessed, like most people who knew her as "Lady Mortimer", that bit of her background was always a surprise.

"When you opened the door of the pub that night, what did you see?" she said.

"Big crowd, noisy. But people had backed away to make some space – Oliver Brown had Ben Carmody by the throat, up hard against the wall, fist up, shouting at him—"

"Shouting what? Could you hear?"

"He said – and I quote – 'Bloody stay away from her or I'll *kill* you, I swear to God, I'll kill you'."

"Those exact words?" said Kat.

Loxley nodded.

No wonder Brown was arrested within hours, thought Kat. *Words like that – tough break for a defence lawyer.*

And pretty clear what the argument was about.

"Nobody else involved?" she said.

"Two of them at it. But some bloke was trying to drag Brown away, calm him down, you know."

"Got a name?"

"Davis. Drinking buddy of theirs."

"Will Davis?" said Kat, recognising the name again.

"That's him. Bloke's a right idiot."

"Oh yes?" said Kat, fishing.

"He'd be in prison too, if I had my way."

"Really? Why?"

"You see, day after we arrested Brown, Davis turned up, signed a statement that Brown had left the pub with him that night."

"A false statement?"

"From beginning to end. Got tripped up right away, soon as we looked into things. Said he did it for his mate. Didn't take us more than a day to find out. Sergeant Timms let him off with a warning. Me – I'd have charged him."

Interesting, Kat thought. *Another good reason to talk to Davis as soon as possible.*

"Okay – back at the pub," she said, "this fella Davis – trying to stop the fight, yes?"

"Trying and failing. Brown's built like an ox."

"And Carmody?"

"Lightweight, in comparison."

"No contest?"

"Not a chance."

"So – you walked in, and Brown saw you, right?"

"*Heard* me first – I made it clear police were on the premises – then he turned and spotted me. Let go of Carmody."

"And that was it? Fight over?"

"They dusted themselves down. Davis said it was just a misunderstanding, set up some beers at the bar. Brown cooled down fast. Said sorry. Even shook hands with Carmody. That, probably for show. But looked like things were over, so I left."

"End of the incident, huh?"

"What I thought. Made a note of the names, then left them to it. Looked like the disagreement was over." Loxley took a breath. "Least the fighting part of it!"

"What time was that?"

"Nine thirty."

"You went back to the police station?"

"No. Finished my rounds. Did another circuit of the town. And – as we all know – ended up here."

"Why this narrow alleyway? You remember why you came up here?"

"No reason. Take different paths, still getting to know the town, the different ways to get around. Sometimes I go the long way round, check the Arundel Road—"

"And the time now—was what?"

"About eleven."

"Pubs close at ten thirty, yes?"

"That's right."

"And that means… by the time you got here, most people in town had gone home?"

"Didn't see a soul once I left the square."

Kat pondered this: so far, nothing unusual in Loxley's report to seize hold of.

But then…

"What do you think Ben Carmody was doing here, in this alley?"

Loxley pointed across the snowy, empty fields. In the distance, Kat was surprised to see the dark outline of Blackmead Farm, smoke curling from a chimney.

On foot the farm was clearly not so far from the village.

"He lives up there. Was on his way home. Regular shortcut across the fields from the pub."

"Blackmead Farm, yes?" said Kat.

"That's right."

"And Brown – where does he live?"

"Other side of town, off the Petersfield Road."

Now that was interesting.

That moment when things just don't add up. Always exciting.

"Then – this would be the wrong direction for Brown, going home?"

"Completely."

"Did the two of them leave the pub together?"

"Spoke to some of the men who were there. More or less, that's what they said. Witnesses aren't consistent and you know—"

"Lot of drink taken, not surprising."

"Yes. But one thing they did agree on – Brown had had a skinful. Falling about."

Skinful.

I'll learn this lingo eventually, Kat thought.

She looked up and down the alleyway, trying to imagine the events of that November night.

Then she noticed something. Maybe something not terribly important, really more of a guess.

But still...

"So, that night, Carmody came walking up here, just as we did now. It's so narrow here, he'd have easily known if someone was following him? Especially if they were drunk, staggering?"

"True. Though he might have invited Brown back to his lodgings for a nightcap."

"After being attacked by him? Seems unlikely, yes?"

"But possible."

"Okay then. But bear with me. Say he's alone, and he comes to this opening. This place... hidden from the village centre. I got to tell you one thing..."

"Go on, Lady Mortimer."

"Look around. This is the perfect spot to wait for someone – knowing they usually take   this shortcut, as Carmody did.

Wait for them, surprise them coming out of the alley. No one likely to see – or even hear."

Kat noticed Loxley's expression change.

"You're right, Lady Mortimer," he said. "Just right for a nasty surprise like that. But then – it still could have been Brown. If he came round fast on the main road."

"True," said Kat. "But you saw him that night. Was Brown in a fit enough state to run ahead and lie in wait? Do you *buy that*?"

"Buy it?"

"Believe that is at all possible?" Kat said.

She watched him look up and down the alley again as if replaying the crime from different angles.

"Okay. Maybe not. But it's all hypothetical, isn't it?" he said. "Whereas the evidence – the real, hard evidence – points to Brown."

"Even though he was falling-over drunk?"

"Easy enough to put on a show, fool that lot down the pub. I mean, if he *was* planning something."

"That's a big 'if', constable. Tell me, where was the murder weapon found?" said Kat.

Loxley nodded. "Brown's back garden, under a bush. Clasp knife."

"Any fingerprints?" said Kat.

"The officer who found it, ahem, mishandled the knife."

Sergeant Timms, no doubt, thought Kat.

"Shame," she said. "What about the shirt?"

"I found that in Brown's vegetable patch, dug in. Drenched in blood it was."

"Not the cleverest place to hide it. Or the knife."

"True."

THE WRONG MAN

"And were you one of the arresting officers?"

"I was there."

"And how did Brown react?"

"He looked surprised. Dopey. Falling over almost. Like maybe he was still drunk."

"Didn't put up a fight?" said Kat, surprised.

"No," said Loxley shaking his head, as if he, too, found Brown's reaction unexpected.

Then he checked his watch. "We done? Sergeant Timms will have had his tea by now." A grin. "Be looking for me, I imagine."

"Yes, sure. This is so helpful. One last thing though," she said. "Just curious. Why did you want to come up here with me this morning? Why help?"

Loxley shrugged. "Dunno. Just interested in how you might see things, I suppose."

"Or maybe you doubt the conviction?"

Loxley paused before answering that one.

Shrewd officer, Kat thought.

"Not my job," said Loxley. "I arrest 'em. I don't judge them."

"But I'm guessing you have an opinion. Don't you?"

She saw him rub his chin, look around as if to check nobody might hear.

"All right," he said. "Between you and me? Promise it'll go no further?"

"Absolutely."

He stepped close. "When we put Brown behind bars, I was, well, thrilled. Really was! Nabbed a killer – barely a day after the crime? Top class policework."

"But?"

"But, since then, I can't help feeling it was all *too* easy. Everything falling into place? The knife. The shirt. And now, see, there's a question, keeps coming back, riling me, waking me in the night…"

"Go on."

"That question: have we all somehow been played?" he said. "Stitched up, you know? Taken for fools. Because, if we have, there's nothing I can do about it. It's too late. So yeah, reckon I thought the only person who can save an innocent man from being hanged – *if* he is innocent – is you."

He looked at her long and hard, then he turned and headed back down the alleyway, disappearing from view.

Leaving Kat, alone in the snow on the edge of town, knowing that Loxley might be right.

But in a sense, he was also wrong.

Because it wasn't all down to her to save Ollie Brown's life.

It was down to Harry too.

As Kat set off through the snow, back into town, she wondered how Harry was getting on in London.

Because, so far, all she'd found were some curious uncertainties.

While all that incriminating evidence remained firmly in place.

THE WRONG MAN

8.

THE CONDEMNED MAN

HARRY JUMPED OUT of the cab, paid the driver, and then turned to take in the forbidding shape of the fortress-like Pentonville Prison.

Although it was just midday, the sky was dark with brooding snow clouds gathering, which didn't augur well for his train journey back to Mydworth later.

A bit of a growl from his stomach, and he realised he'd not had a bite to eat since breakfast.

No time for lunch: a two-hour meeting at the Foreign Office, followed by some discussion with his boss about a proposed meeting in the South of France (*Good opportunity to squeeze in a little jaunt with Kat perhaps*, he thought).

And then a rush across town to Lincoln's Inn Fields where an old school pal (who had chambers there) had called in a favour and arranged access for Harry to one of Brown's defence team juniors.

But though Harry had been able to read more details on the case, he was none the wiser as to any grounds for a further appeal. He'd never read anything more open-and-shut.

Now he was here to meet the condemned man, and see if Brown himself might provide a thread to – somehow – unpick the looming hangman's rope.

He crossed the pavement and approached the prison guard on duty at the entrance.

"Sir Harry Mortimer, to see the Governor," he said.

He watched the guards retreat to the cabin by the gates, check the log book, then return and unlock the tall, heavy iron gates that *clanked* with a solemn finality.

"This way, sir," said the guard, and Harry slipped through, then followed him into Pentonville Prison.

"MUST TELL YOU, Sir Harry, I'm quite surprised the Intelligence services have an *angle* on Brown," said the Governor, as he led Harry from the prison offices, through a maze of locked gates into "A" Wing, where the condemned man – and the gallows – awaited.

Harry didn't respond. He knew the Governor – clearly an old hand – wasn't expecting an answer anyway.

Harry's clearance in a small secretive offshoot of the Foreign Office had given him privileged access – no questions asked – to Brown on death row.

So, he'd told a white lie that Brown was "a person of interest". He'd felt it served no purpose to say his visit was a last-ditch attempt to find evidence that might delay the hanging.

Moving through one last set of locked gates, they now entered "A" Wing. The long, Victorian building with its open staircases, metal gantries and lines of cells three stories high, echoed to their footsteps.

Otherwise the place felt – to Harry – uncannily quiet.

"Visited us before, old chap?" said the Governor.

"Why, yes. I was here in '25 to observe an execution," said Harry, the grim memory of that day returning.

A foreign spy whom Harry had helped to nail, paying the ultimate price for his treachery.

"Bit more civilised now since we did the place up a bit, I'm sure you'll agree," said the Governor cheerily.

Harry recalled a primitive shed out in the prison yard, and the long walk the prisoner had to make to the gallows.

"Moved the whole *show* inside," said the Governor, stopping at a staircase by a section of the wing separated from the rest, then leading Harry up the first flight of steps. "Modernised, you see," he said, as they emerged and Harry saw a line of prison doors with small windows, and a prison guard on a small folding chair outside one.

"So, there are two condemned cells. The gallows room sits nice and tidy in between them – though the poor beggars don't realise that until the last minute."

Harry wondered if that was a warning to him *not to spoil the surprise?*

"Here we are," said the Governor. "I imagine you won't want a guard with you?"

"No, thank you," said Harry. "I'll be fine."

He waited while the guard took keys from a loop on his belt and unlocked the metal prison door.

The door swung open, and Harry peered in – the cell bigger than he'd expected, and Brown not yet in view.

"Just give us a shout when you're done," said the Governor.

Harry nodded, then entered the cell. And as the door was pulled shut behind him, he saw Oliver Brown sitting at a table in the corner, staring at the grey prison wall.

Looking very much like a doomed man.

"Oliver," he said.

But Brown didn't respond, his broad shoulders hunched, his arms held tight to his chest as if he was in a straitjacket.

Harry could imagine how the bulk, the sheer strength, of this man could be intimidating. And how with all that force he could easily be responsible for the fierce, almost inhuman, attack on Carmody.

He paused for a second – knowing this was going to be difficult – then walked over to the table, gently dragged a chair across, and sat opposite him.

"Oliver," he said again, softly.

He watched as slowly Brown turned from the wall and stared at him: as if only now was he aware that someone had come into the room.

"I'm Harry Mortimer." A pause. "And I'm here to help."

"HARRY MORTIMER?" said Brown, his eyes narrowing. "Sir Harry, from the big house?"

For a second, Harry tensed as he watched Brown sit up, stare at him.

This chap could do me a lot of damage before they get that door open to help me, he thought.

Then he nodded, and Brown laughed. "I know you!"

Harry stared back at him, surprised.

"Harry Mortimer!" said Brown again, rocking back on his chair. "I got you out back in '19, that gentlemen vs players game? Up on the field, when we all came home from France. You weren't half bad, hit a couple of sixes. But you didn't see my slow ball coming, did you? Ha ha! Bought it hook, line and sinker, you did!"

THE WRONG MAN

And Harry suddenly remembered that cricket match ten years ago, so unreal after the horrors of the Front, the villagers crowding the boundary, the soft summer evening, a younger Brown bearing down on him as he batted, each ball whistling past his ears.

"Brown! Of course – yes, I remember you!" he said, laughing at the memory. "How the *hell* did you do that?"

"My lips are sealed! Sent your middle stump flying though, didn't it!"

"It did indeed!" said Harry. "Never lived it down! All we needed was one more run, but I blew it."

"I can see you now – still looking for the ball in the air, umpire already telling you to go. I got no end of pints bought for me that night, I can tell ya!"

Harry laughed again – and for a few seconds the two of them were back in the pavilion at Mydworth Cricket Club, young men from opposite ends of the village, opposite lives, but bound together in one glorious peacetime memory.

Then… the memory suddenly disappeared into thin air.

"Give anything to be back there now, I can tell you," said Brown.

"I'm sure," said Harry.

He leaned forward, feeling there was no need for artifice now; he could just ask the questions as they came to him. "So, what the hell *happened*, Oliver? What are you doing here? *Why*?"

"Beats me," said Oliver. "All been a bit of a blur, really."

Harry took his time with the next question.

"Did you do it? Did you kill Ben Carmody?"

Brown's voice rose at that.

"Course I *didn't*. He was my best mate. Fact, I hope they find out who did, because if I'm still around I'll damn well kill him, I will, I swear."

Harry shot a look at the jail cell door.

"You'd better not say *that* too loud, or you'll be back here again – and they'll hang you twice!" said Harry, and, impossibly, they both laughed at this.

"But seriously, Oliver, what *did* happen? I mean, the evidence against you... I've seen it, old chap. I would convict you too if I were on the jury."

"I know, it's a right old mess. None of it makes sense. Trouble is, Sir Harry – when I try and piece together what happened that night, my mind just goes blank."

"What do you mean? You can't remember, or you don't want to? That can happen, you know, when something terrible occurs. The mind just goes into shock—"

"No, no, it's not like that. It's something else. See – I know me and Ben had a go at each other in the pub that night. Bit of pushing and shoving."

Oliver looked away. "About to come to blows, we was. But then that copper turned up? Had a word with us, calmed us down. And my mate Will, well he got us laughing again. Then he bought a round. We even had a game of darts."

Harry knew that everything Oliver Brown was telling him could be easily checked.

And none of it fit the picture of man planning on stabbing someone to death.

"But then, see, next thing I remember, I'm in the cell in Mydworth Police Station, biggest headache I ever had."

"You seriously don't remember anything in between?"

"Nothing – nothing at all."

THE WRONG MAN

"Sounds to me like you just had a few too many pints?"

"Had some, sure. But wasn't that. I *know* it wasn't that. I never, in all my years, had no hangover like that, *never*."

Harry looked at him: the poor man so confused, so lost, desperately trying to retrieve memories that might rescue him.

"So, you don't even remember leaving the pub?"

"No."

"Getting home?"

"No. Though Mabel says it was a while after closing time."

"But you don't know where you were?"

"That's just the thing! Not a clue."

"For that whole time?"

"No."

Harry sat back. Again, it was no wonder the jury voted as one.

Brown had no defence at all.

"Ollie," said Harry, leaning close, "you don't think maybe you got angry with Carmody, went after him, lost your temper?" A breath. "Did him in?"

Harry expected the man to rise to that. But he just shrugged.

"*Listen.* I don't think I did. But who knows? Maybe I went mad. Maybe that's what really happened! Went mad and killed my best pal."

Harry leaned across, put a hand on Brown's forearm.

"If it's any comfort, Oliver, I don't believe that for one minute. I'm starting to believe you might just be innocent."

"You are?" said Brown, raising his head and looking at Harry as if in wonder.

"I am," said Harry. "Despite all that evidence. But if you're a God-fearing man, you'd better start praying. Because there isn't much time to fix this. Couple of days, that's all

58

we have. You need to tell me everything that you *do* remember."

He saw Brown sit up again, wipe his chin, as if resolving to help.

"You really think you can get me out of this mess?" said Brown. "I've already lost the appeal, you know that? They even weighed me for the drop. I ain't never heard of anyone coming back from a hanging as late in the day as this."

"There's always a first time," said Harry. "We'll go through it now, from the beginning, all over again. I want you to tell me everything you know about Ben Carmody – and about why you were fighting. Because maybe there's something that happened that night that just might get you out of this place. I promise you this: I'm going to try my damnedest."

He watched Oliver take this in – the man thinking the case wasn't totally lost.

And something told Harry that if he listened, *really listened* to this account, there might be an idea, the merest *seed* of an idea that could save the man from his appointment with the hangman.

9.

THE STATION INN

KAT SAT IN the Alvis in the station car park, engine running to keep warm, and watched the London train pull in late, the steam and smoke swirling among the falling snow in great clouds, brightly lit by the light from the gas lamps on the station platform.

She heard the carriage doors slam, then with a whistle, the great steam engine pulled away, wheels screeching on the frozen tracks.

Weather like this, she thought, *amazing the train is running at all.*

A few figures emerged into the car park, huddled low against the now-driving snow. Finally, she saw Harry and tooted the car's horn.

"Boy, am I glad to see you," he said, opening the passenger door of the Alvis, shaking off the snow and climbing into the front seat. "Sorry you've had to wait."

"Least I could do," said Kat, as he leaned across for a kiss. "Your nose is cold."

"And you – my dear – are wonderfully warm."

She saw a sparkle in his dark eyes.

"Well, Sir Harry, I wouldn't get *too* comfortable," said Kat. "There's somewhere we need to go before we head home."

"Let me guess. The Station Inn?" said Harry.

"You thought so too?"

"Oh, yes. Definitely. Seven o'clock, perfect time to grab any regulars who might have been around that night."

"Your meeting with Oliver Brown… anything?"

"Well, good news and bad news," said Harry. "Good news – I think there may be a chance that our boy Oliver is innocent."

"And – let me guess – that's also the bad news?"

"*Exactly*. Quick catch-up?"

With the car heater doing its best to keep them warm, new snow clumping on the windshield, Kat told him about her visit to Ben Carmody's lodgings in the dilapidated Blackmead Farm, followed by her morning with Timms and Loxley.

"Loxley sounds useful," said Harry when she'd finished.

"Sharper than Timms, that's for sure."

"What about the solicitor?"

"In the end, I phoned him. Said he was quite happy for us to take a second look at the case. But hardly optimistic."

"I don't blame him," said Harry. And Kat listened as he went through the details he'd picked up from the barrister's junior.

"So, no leads there," she said.

"Nope."

"And Pentonville?" Kat said. "I'm very curious. Never been in a British jail."

"Not at all convivial. Best avoided, in my opinion. I didn't learn a great deal more about what happened at the pub. But I *did* – more or less – find out what the row with Ben Carmody was about."

"*La femme?*" said Kat. "It's always about la femme, isn't it?"

THE WRONG MAN

"*Vraiment*," said Harry. "*Cherchez*, as they say. Oh, that reminds me – you will positively love this – the office wants me to go to Nice for a week, debrief some chap who's been undercover in North Africa. Fancy coming along for the fun?"

"The Riviera? Really? Do you even have to ask?"

"We can stay at the Negresco."

"Your favourite hotel. Can't wait, darling. Now – back to *la femme?*"

"Ah, yes. Well, seems Ben and Oliver and Mabel all grew up together here in Mydworth. Ben apparently courted Mabel for a year or two but it was Oliver who won fair maid in the end."

"How romantic," said Kat.

"Indeed. Anyway, for some reason, Oliver got it into his head in the summer that Mabel and Ben were having a bit of a fling again."

"Oh dear. Classic stuff. When it comes to murder, that is. But how did he get that idea?"

"Not at all sure. He did admit that he and Ben had a few run-ins, nothing serious until that night."

"Any idea why it got serious?"

"Oliver told me he heard a rumour that Mabel and Ben had been seen canoodling in the Green Man the week before, while he was working."

"A rumour?" said Kat. "You think it happened?"

"Who knows? But, when he heard about it, Oliver apparently blew his top. And I suspect that the lad does have a top to blow."

"And the rest of the story we know – or think we know."

"Right. But where'd that rumour come from? We need to chat to Mabel again," said Harry. "And also Ollie's pal, this Will Davis—"

"Loxley mentioned him," said Kat. "Said he tried to calm the friends down. Even gave Brown a false alibi to try and get him off the hook."

"Really? Well, that's interesting. So *many* interesting things about this open-and-shut case. Tell me, did the police charge him?"

"No."

"Lucky chap."

"Right. What I thought as well. Anyway, seems he's a regular at the Station Inn."

"Oliver told me that too."

"So – what are we waiting for?" said Kat, turning the engine off. "Let's walk up to the pub, find some witnesses, come back for the car."

"Oh dear. Out into the cold again? Well, anything in the cause of justice," said Harry, popping his hat back on and climbing out.

Together, arm in arm in the falling snow, they walked back up the road towards the village, over the old bridge, to the Station Inn, the rough-and-ready pub which – tonight at least, thought Kat – looked *almost* romantic in the falling snow.

HARRY PUSHED OPEN the door of the pub expecting the place to be crowded.

After all, the Station Inn was the watering hole for the new factories on the other side of the railway line. Workers would drop in "for a quick one" on the way home. Some for quite a few more than a "quick" one.

But tonight Harry could see barely a dozen drinkers seated at tables: just a couple of labourers at the bar; a few games of cribbage going on; in the corner, a bookish looking young man reading the paper, pipe in hand.

He and Kat went to the bar where a brawny barman with rolled-up sleeves and tattooed forearms – a massive anchor on one arm, a giant "Mother" inscribed in a heart on the other – was wiping mugs with a cloth.

"Two pints of mild, please, barman," said Harry. "And one for yourself."

The barman nodded, and Harry could see him assessing these two strangers – especially the woman expecting to drink a pint… right here!

"Kind of you, sir," said the barman, filling the first pint. "I'll put it in the *wood*, if you don't mind."

The drinks came and Harry clinked glasses with Kat, then they both drank.

"You the landlord?" said Harry as the barman resumed his pot wiping, surveying his domain.

"I am," said the man, and Harry heard a note of suspicion in his voice. "Freddie Fry."

The barman probably thinking: W*ho've we got here then? Excise, tax, police, licensing…?*

"Mind me asking… were you behind the bar the night Oliver Brown was in here?"

The barman slowed his efforts at polishing, attention caught.

"You mean the night Ben Carmody was done for?" said the landlord.

Harry nodded.

"And *who* would be asking?" said the man, putting his cloth and mug down and stepping   closer. "Not journalists, I hope.

Because, you see, I don't *like* journalists. And if you two are *journalists* there's the damn door and you'll be going through it on the end of my boot. You too, madam."

"Oh, don't hold back on my account, Mr Fry," said Kat. "I'm all for equality. Though I'd recommend you be careful with any of that 'boot' talk around my husband here. My boots are pretty tough too, you know."

"A Yank," the barman said doing nothing to hide his disdain.

Harry laughed. "Oh, you've *got* her there, Mr Fry – well-spotted! But no, we're not journalists. Though I should also warn you – seriously – don't get on the wrong side of my wife here. Trust me. Her bite? Much, much worse than her bark."

He saw the landlord force a smile, but tension was still in the air. Harry leaned forward, closing the gap between them.

"So, here's the thing, you see. Oliver Brown is set to hang for the crime of murder at dawn on Friday, as I'm sure you know. And my wife and I are trying to find any missing evidence that could save him from the gallows."

"Private investigators?"

"No. Interesting thought, that, but just, er, well-wishers."

"Do-gooders you mean?"

"Maybe," said Kat. "Anything wrong with that?"

"Who's paying you?"

"Nobody. We're very affordable do-gooders, you see."

The barman seemed to consider the idea. "All right. Used to like old Ollie. How can I help?"

"Jolly good," said Harry. "Back to square one, as they say. Were you here that night?"

"I was."

"And you saw what happened?"

THE WRONG MAN

"I did."

Pulling teeth, thought Harry. *Come on, man!*

"You know Oliver – and Ben?" said Kat.

"Sure. Regulars, they were."

Harry glanced at Kat, wondering how many *days* it would take to drag some relevant information out of this man. But then a voice from behind them:

"Regulars – yes. And usually, regular *gentlemen,* the pair of them."

Harry turned, to see the bookish young man from the corner, standing, newspaper clamped under one arm, pipe in one hand – and the other hand outstretched to shake theirs.

"Will Davis," said the man. "I'm a friend of Oliver's."

Harry took the man's hand to shake, about to introduce himself, but Will beat him to it.

"Sir Harry and Lady Mortimer, if I'm not mistaken," he said.

"You got it," said Kat. "But how—"

Will smiled. "Whole town knows what you're up to," said Will.

"That right?" said Harry, not sure how to take this news. "And here I thought we were being ever so discreet."

"Oh, I wouldn't worry," said Will. "Best thing that could have happened. Only chance we've got of seeing justice done. Not that we've got much time, of course."

"Indeed," said Harry. "In fact – we were hoping to have a little chat with you about that night, if you don't mind."

"Mind? Dear me no, I've been wanting to talk to you too."

"Now a good time?" said Kat.

"*Absolutely,*" said Will. He turned and gestured towards his seat in the corner.

"Look – got a nice cosy spot there, bring your drinks, ask what you will, I only hope somehow I can help."

Harry looked at Kat who nodded.

Maybe now they might get somewhere…

THE WRONG MAN

10.

WHAT WILL SAW

KAT SAT OPPOSITE Will Davis, taking him in as Harry brought a new round of drinks to the table.

In his late twenties perhaps, he had the slightly tousled air of an academic, though his tweed jacket and twill trousers looked to be good quality. Horn-rimmed glasses suggested timidity, but a bright bow tie and matching kerchief in his top pocket gave him a bit of a dashing air.

Not from Mydworth, she thought. *Far too cosmopolitan.*

Which turned out to be right.

"So, Will, do you work in Mydworth?" Harry asked.

"Oh no. Not really. I'm an insurance salesman," said Davis, laughing. "Consolidated Mutual. Lot of travelling around, you see. So, beware, I'll have you two signed up for a life policy before you know it!"

"Just passing through, then?" said Harry, smiling.

"Been based here for the last six months. Originally from Manchester, via Cambridge. Head office is up in London but, luckily, I don't have to go there much. Imagine, in this weather!"

"Sounds like a nice little job," said Kat.

"Oh, it is," said Will. "I absolutely *love* it! Roaming the south of England in the old Austin, selling policies, my destiny in my own hands, the freedom of the road!

'Freelance' they call it. *Free lance* – like a knight of yore, you see?"

"Doing good deeds, saving maidens?" said Kat.

"Ha, yes, that's me – occasionally!" said Will, his eyes twinkling.

Kat could imagine how attractive his spiel was. *Guy could sell policies on that smile alone,* she thought.

"You have a house here?" said Harry.

"Just lodgings. A very pleasant room with private bathroom at the residence of the very elderly, very deaf – and very nosy – Mrs Pinder, on Crab Tree Lane. One guinea a week, all in, breakfast included, no guests. Especially *no* guests – she was quite clear about *that* point!"

He laughed again, then tapped out his pipe, scraped the bowl with a pocket knife, and started filling it from an old leather pouch.

"But look, we're not here to talk about me, are we? We're here to try and save a good man from an untimely death at the hands of the hangman. I assume, like me, you are convinced that Oliver is innocent?"

Kat looked at Harry, then back at Davis.

"We are starting to think so. Though, so far, the evidence isn't cooperating."

"I know," said Davis. "But, ask me what you will. *Fire away.* And let us, all three, hope that there's something in what I tell you that might stop this dreadful miscarriage of justice."

KAT SAW HARRY lean back, and she took that as a signal that she should begin the questioning.

"Will, that night, was anything out of the ordinary?"

THE WRONG MAN

Another puff, and he shrugged. "No. A normal Saturday night at the local. Place busy: darts, laughter, smoke…" He took the pipe out of his mouth, a half-smile. "Did my bit there. So, no, nothing unusual."

Kat nodded at that. Will seemed affable, eager to help.

"But sooner or later things turned nasty, yes? An argument broke out, between Oliver and Ben?"

Will's eyes lowered at that, as if his memory was now becoming overcast with the recollection of how the evening turned.

And it's just that "turn" I'm interested in, Kat thought.

"Well, yes." A small smile crept onto Will's face. "You know how it is with pals, out for the night, all those pints? I mean, is there a pub in all of England where a fight *doesn't* break out on a Saturday night?"

Kat nodded. Will seemed weary of the inevitable violence. Almost… *philosophical.*

Based on Harry's description of Oliver Brown, Will seemed a strange choice for a friend. Though perhaps the real connection was through Ben, who had moved on to a different life from his old farmhand friend.

"Well, you know, Will," she said, "I spent a lot of Saturday nights working in a bar in the Bronx. Saw my share of fights break out. Comes with the territory."

Kat saw Will fire a glance at Harry, as if she might be having him on.

"Really? You worked in a pub?"

"Yes. My dad's place. And while we didn't get many farm workers in the Bronx – well *any* – still, the crowd, I imagine, not that much different than here? But here's my point. Those fights I helped break up with my dad – they didn't just come out of *nowhere.*"

Will didn't respond to that.

"No matter how many bats and balls the crowd had."

Will's eyes widened as he leaned close.

"Excuse me? Bats and–?"

Kat laughed. "A shot with a beer chaser. We like our baseball as much as our drinks."

"Interesting."

For a moment she thought Will might extract a notebook to scrawl down the just-learned Americanism.

Like a linguist in the wild doing research.

"See – there was always *something* that lit that fire… got the argument going. An old grudge, grievance, a slight from a long time ago – or yesterday."

Kat leaned forward.

"So, that fight. Oliver… Ben. Where did it come from? What was the 'match' that set it off?"

APPROPRIATELY, WILL'S PIPE sputtered out to a last little puff, and he dug out his pouch, gave it a quick refill – a light, and he was back in business.

Kat used the moment to take a sip of her beer. The ale more bitter than the brands sold at the Lucky Shamrock back in New York.

And definitely warmer.

While Will puffed, Harry took the opportunity to add, looking at Kat, "You were there, Will? Just before it happened."

With the additional nudge, Will nodded. But Kat could see that his earlier keenness had diminished.

"Yes," he finally said. "I was. But this 'match' you are asking about? Look, I really don't like talking about other people's *personal* affairs, you know. Their business is *their* business."

"Understandable," Kat said. "But Oliver's life is at stake here."

She watched him as he wrestled with his unease. Then he shrugged.

"Okay. I knew that Ben and Ollie went way back. And that somehow in the middle of it all was Mabel." Will looked at Harry, then back to her. "Maybe you two know all about that."

Cherchez la femme, indeed, thought Kat.

"I thought that was all ancient history. Ollie and Mabel have a beautiful little girl. Ben was doing well with the electrical work. 'Riding the wave of the future', is what I always said to them."

"But something came up that night?" Kat said.

"Well, yes, out of nowhere, really. I mean, I could tell Ollie seemed tense. Drinking a bit too fast, you know?"

Kat nodded.

"Ben seemed his old self. But then Ollie got angry. Said something about something he had heard. Not sure how. Just a rumour, I suppose. Maybe from one of the chaps he worked with? Some blokes like to stir up trouble. You know the Green Man?"

Kat nodded.

"Ollie claimed that Ben had been seen there, with Mabel."

"Go on," Harry said quietly.

"Well, you can imagine. Hell broke loose, it did. Ben exploded, denied the whole thing, and then he got angry that

Ollie would even *think* that. Course, my role in the evening suddenly changed."

"Peacemaker?" Kat said.

"An attempt at least. But it all took *seconds*, you see? A flash-fire, and Ollie – he was at Ben's throat, a big hand wrapped around, and me—" Will shook his head at this "—stuck in the middle. Tell you, I had my work cut out for me."

"Did the barman help?"

"Dear old Freddie? Think he called the police when he saw the first fist raised. The whole thing was about to spill outside for a full-on battle… but then the constable walked in. Said a few words, and suddenly it ended."

Kat saw on Harry's face that he wasn't sure about something.

"*Ended?* Just like that?"

"Funny thing is, *it did*. I suppose the threat of a night in jail worked. Anyway, I took the chance to buy a round, get the party back on."

As Kat listened to this, a few things didn't make sense to her.

"Hang on. Oliver was able to just *let go* of all that suspicion?"

"Maybe he decided a rumour was just a rumour? Anyway, he went quiet, and all that fierceness vanished. Remarkable really."

Will put down his pipe.

Yes, indeed, thought Kat. *And unfortunately, it fitted quite well with the theory that Oliver could let go of that anger… because he already had murderous plans for later.*

THE WRONG MAN

Harry pulled his chair close. Voice lowered, a look to the other tables, barrelling on with the drinks, smokes and hearty laughs.

"Will – now we get to perhaps the most important part of the evening. What happened when Ben and Ollie left."

11.

THE MOMENTS BEFORE A MURDER

Harry thought that whatever Will knew about the next minutes – the next hour – might be key to understanding Ben's murder.

"I gather you left before Ben and Ollie?" he said.

Will nodded. "Once I'd bought the round, and the two of them were more or less back to normal, I felt, well, my work was done. Had a big trip coming up next day, so an early night suited me. I also thought, once the pub closed, Ben would go his way, Ollie his."

"And what state were they in then?"

"Not too far gone. When I left, at least. But, word is, when Oliver finally walked out, he looked *wobbly* as hell. Must have been hitting the stuff hard. Maybe you heard that too?"

Harry didn't indicate one way or the other. He saw Kat had her eyes fixed on the man.

"Apparently Ollie staggered out first, ready to sail home. Ben lingered a bit."

"That's odd," Kat said.

Will cocked his head in her direction.

"Odd, Lady Mortimer?"

"Yes. Oliver Brown leaves ahead of Ben. Heads home. And yet he doesn't get home until sometime later."

Will frowned, as if not understanding the implications.

"Plenty of time in fact," Kat added, "for Oliver to go down to Slip-Knot Alley, find a place to hide, and just wait for Ben. And there you are."

Harry saw Will lick his lips at the unsavoury logic of it all.

"I for one *never* believed that. I think he fell down, dozed a bit then dragged himself home."

"Maybe," Kat said with no real assurance.

"Just one final thing, Will. One last question."

"Of course."

"Why did you lie to the police? Why give Oliver a false alibi?"

HARRY WATCHED AS Will looked away, the mood on his face unreadable.

Taking his time, Harry thought.

"When I moved to this village, all those months ago, I didn't really know anyone." He nodded to the bar. "Then I started coming here, meeting the regulars. Kind of place where you can be left to your own devices, or not. But you know pubs... Well, Sir Harry, maybe you don't."

Harry turned to Kat, smiled.

"Oh, no worries on that account."

Will laughed.

"So, I met Ben. And then, through Ben, Ollie. Seemed to me at first rather a strange pair to be pals."

Kat leaned forward at that.

"What do you mean? Strange?"

"Well, Ben had – you know – made something of himself. Basically, he ran that little electrical shop for the owner. He often said to me he hoped that it might become his business one day, if things went well."

"And Ollie?" Kat asked.

"Nice chap. I mean, a jolly good sort. 'Salt of the earth', is the expression I'd use. Hard working lad. But – see – that's just the thing. I doubt Ollie had any real aspirations... or hopes."

"A mismatch you think?" Harry said.

"To a stranger like me, when I first got here? Yes. But then, I got to know them and I realised. They had *history*. Grew up together. Worked together as lads. And that's the important thing when it comes to being pals."

"And you didn't feel like an outsider?" said Kat.

"On the contrary. That was the special thing about them, you see. They made me feel like I was an old pal too."

Harry saw Will look down at his beer, eyes moist. He waited for a few seconds, so the chap could pull himself together.

"Sorry about that," said Will, taking his handkerchief from his top pocket and blowing his nose. "Like I said – good pals."

"Don't worry," said Harry. "So, the police asked you about that night."

"Yes. And well, I knew that Ollie couldn't possibly have done that to Ben. So, I said I met up with Ollie outside the pub, then walked home with him. Seemed the obvious thing to do. To help out a friend?"

Harry looked at Kat. This territory more hers than his.

"But the story didn't hold water?"

A sheepish grin from Will. "No. Stupid of me really."

"And why didn't your statement stand up?"

"Oh… Dear old Mrs Pinder heard me come in, that's why," said Will. "Typical! Seems I made a bit of noise. I mean, we had been at it all evening."

"You were lucky that Timms didn't decide to press charges against you," said Harry. "Lying to the police, even in the service of a good friend, is still a crime."

"Yes. Idiotic, I know. And, well, it didn't work."

Harry still had one last question. But then it turned out his wife did as well.

Exactly the same question…

"Will, if you felt Ollie didn't commit the murder… then who did?"

"Who did it? Sorry, I'm not a detective. I couldn't even begin to guess."

"No idea at all?"

Harry waited, until Will finally spoke.

"Ben worked all over this area – everything from setting up new appliances to full-on electrical installations. What if he crossed paths with someone? Did something happen? Some hidden history that led to someone wanting him dead? I mean, that *could* be it. But it beats me what that could be."

As Harry listened he thought, *There's a certain logic to Davis's words.*

But, by every account, Ben wasn't someone who made enemies like that. And even if it was true, it could take weeks to unearth this mystery person – if he even existed.

And Oliver Brown was due to hang in two days.

"Well, getting late," Will said, checking his wristwatch again. "Busy day tomorrow. Full day of appointments in Brighton, early start, I'd best—"

Harry quickly smiled as Davis made to get up.

"Will, I – *we* – want to thank you. All this – very helpful."

Will smiled back weakly.

"You really think you've got a chance of saving Ollie?" he said. "Honestly?"

Harry looked at Kat, then back at Will.

"All I can say is – we'll do our very best."

"He's innocent, you know," said Will. "It's a damn shame."

And with a final nod he sailed out of the pub.

Leaving Harry and Kat alone.

"PENNY FOR YOUR thoughts?" said Kat, as she drained her glass and set it on the table.

"Right price, I'd say. Not sure they're worth much more," said Harry.

"Things look bad for Oliver, don't they?"

"And Mabel… the little girl. Terrible. The clock's ticking."

"Dawn, the day after tomorrow," said Kat. "Time running out."

"*And* options."

"Let's get out of here, shall we? Go through those options."

"Good idea. Quick dash home; dinner waiting for us, if memory serves."

"Cocktails first? Loosen some brain cells?"

"I *do* like the way your mind works," said Harry. "You really could be one of those – what do they call them? – mindreaders."

"When it comes to your preferences, I have that *all* covered."

Harry got up and went to the nearby coat rack to retrieve their heavy coats.

"Tell me, are all American women so insightful?"

"When it comes to men, I'd say yes."

"What a country! Button up by the way – my guess is we've dropped a few degrees in the past hour."

Harry took her arm and led the way out of the smoke-filled pub.

Outside, the snow sparkled like tiny crystals on the road.

"Brrr," Sir Harry said. "Cannot wait for those cocktails. Fireside I'd suggest."

It was cold but, with Kat tight by his side, he was not at all shivery.

And as they walked to their parked Alvis.

"Kat, I do feel I've let Oliver Brown down. Do you feel the same?"

"Yes. But I guess, like we said to Will, we are doing our best—"

Harry felt her lean into him even closer, the two of them nearly one figure against the bitter wind.

In the quiet street, the town of Mydworth all burrowed away from the snow and ice, he picked up the pace.

IN THE FRONT seat of the Alvis, Kat pulled her coat tight, as Harry guided the car carefully through the streets towards home.

To Kat, the snowy scene looked like a Hollywood version of a wintry English village: the warm glow of street lamps, the windows of the Kings Arms steamed up, a couple of locals, heads down against the wind, plodding home across the town square.

As Harry drove up the High Street in silence, concentrating hard as the car slithered on the icy cobbles, he paused at the junction by the church, just outside the Green Man, to let another vehicle slowly pass by.

Kat looked at the pub through the misted side window of the Alvis: remembering, it was here that Ben Carmody's rumoured assignation with Mabel had taken place.

Inside the pub – much more *genteel* than the Station Inn – a handful of brave souls stood at the bar. In one corner, she could see through a narrow gap in the curtains, a couple sitting close together, their backs to the window, the man's arm round the woman's waist.

"Tomorrow, we should go back and talk to Mabel," she said, but not turning to Harry. "See if we can track down just where that rumour about her and Ben came from."

"Think it might be important?"

"We've only got a day left, Harry. No stone unturned, remember?"

She felt the tyres fighting for grip as the Alvis began to pull away uphill, and as the car moved, the small change of angle suddenly revealed a different view of the couple in the pub.

And Kat could barely believe her eyes.

"Harry, stop!"

He hit the brakes, the Alvis slid on the icy road.

"What is it?" he said, turning to her, looking concerned.

"In the pub. Right there. The man and the woman in the corner."

"Well, I'll be damned," Harry said as Kat saw him lean forward, peering past her through the half-misted passenger window. "Will Davis, the crafty devil! Thought he said he had an early start!"

THE WRONG MAN

"That's not the point," said Kat. "Take a closer look. Do you see the woman?"

"I do. You know who she is?"

"Oh yes," said Kat. "That's Connie Price — the housekeeper at Blackmead Farm."

"What? But I thought she——"

As Harry spoke, the couple drained their glasses and stood.

And Kat watched as Will Davis — as if some instinct were in play — turned to look out of the window, through the curtains, directly at the Alvis.

At Kat and Harry.

Kat quickly dropped lower in her seat, and Harry let out the clutch, so the car instantly moved on, past the pub and around the corner.

"You think he saw us?" said Harry, as they turned just seconds later into the drive of the Dower House.

"I don't know," said Kat. "Maybe. Maybe not."

They pulled up in front of the house and Harry turned off the engine. Then they sat in silence for a few seconds.

"So — what the hell does that mean?" said Harry at last.

"Could mean a lot of things. Could be the break we're looking for."

"I agree," said Harry. "Let's get into the warm — and see if we can work it out."

And as they climbed out of the Alvis, Kat's mind was already buzzing with theories about Will Davis's relationship with Connie Price.

And how it might connect with Oliver Brown, and his appointment with the hangman's noose...

12.

A BREAK AT LAST

HARRY OPENED THE drinks cabinet in the sitting room, while Kat checked on the dinner in the kitchen.

"Maggie's done us proud," said Kat, coming in. He watched her flop onto the sofa by the fire. "Just heating it up now. Should be ready in half an hour."

"*Perfect* timing," said Harry, offering up the cocktail shaker for her choice. "Your usual martini? I'm having a scotch by the way. The Macallan."

"Know what?" said Kat, and he saw her kick off her heels and tuck her legs under. "I'll join you. Night like this."

He poured the drinks into two of the best crystal tumblers, then took them over and sat on the armchair facing her.

"To a lucky break," he said, raising his glass.

"*We hope*," said Kat, clinking glasses and taking a sip. "Because we've got around 24 hours left to crack this, Harry. If that."

"I know. So, what do you think about tonight's little development?"

"I think Connie Price deliberately kept Will out of the story she told me. Now there might be a perfectly innocent explanation for that – and said explanation might have

nothing to do with Ben and Ollie. But my instinct is...
somehow it does."

"Well, I do so trust those instincts of yours," said Harry.
"Will also didn't mention he had any link to Ben's household
at all. And – he lied about needing to get home early tonight.
Again – as you say – could be innocent. But *my* instinct..."

Kat took another sip of the Macallan. "Okay – let's act on
those instincts of ours. Dig up everything we can on Will
Davis, background, work, history. Talk to Mabel again – but
push her real hard on Ben, Will – even Connie."

"Absolutely."

"Find out if there's any truth in that rumour about her and
Ben. Gloves off, this time, agree?"

"Yes. I'll have a word with the landlord at the Green
Man," said Harry. "I know the chap. He's got a sharp eye and
a sharp memory. Plus, perhaps I might be able to get a little...
privileged information."

"Too late to do anything tonight, I suppose?" said Kat.

"Maybe not," said Harry. "I can put a call into the office
now. Overnight desk... someone always there. Make it top
priority. Have someone locate the boss of Consolidated
Insurance – first thing in the morning. Get them to open up
their employee files on Will Davis first thing."

"There, you see, Harry – like I said – you *do* have strings
you can pull in London."

"There'll be hell to pay later, don't you worry," said Harry,
laughing. "Misuse of powers, that's what they like to call it.
Hardly a matter of national security, this."

"No," said Kat. "But arguably more important. A man's
life."

"*Indeed*. If a clandestine meeting in a pub really does
connect to our wrong conviction, of course. But we

mustn't forget – it may be no more than that. Just another romantic assignation in sleepy old Mydworth."

"It may be exactly that," said Kat, finishing her whisky and getting up. "But I think I'll sleep a fraction better tonight believing that what we saw is important. The break we've been looking for."

"We can only hope. I'll make that call. Then let's eat. And then – early to bed?"

KAT POURED HERSELF another coffee, picked up her slice of toast, then paused as the grandfather clock in the hallway behind them struck seven.

She looked across the breakfast table at Harry, as behind him, through the sunroom window, the first flickers of dawn light appeared.

"This time tomorrow," she said.

"I know," said Harry.

"In the end, I couldn't sleep. Kept waking, thinking about it. Poor Oliver. I wonder if *he's* awake now."

Harry stretched across the table and squeezed her hand. And then the telephone rang.

She watched Harry race to the phone in the hall, then waited, listening to the murmur of his voice, trying to interpret the news from his words.

After a lifetime, it seemed, he came back into the sunroom and sat again, opposite her.

"Well?" she said. "Who was it? Come on Harry, don't do this to me."

"The office," said Harry. "Seems our chaps roused the Chairman of Consolidated from bed in his club last night.

THE WRONG MAN

Imagine that? And he directly called the Managing Director, who called the London Manager, who called the Head of Personnel, who went to the Consolidated Offices in the Strand, examined the employment files…"

"And?!"

"Turns out there is *not* a salesman named 'Davis'. Indeed, there are *no* so-called freelance agents for Consolidated and never have been. His whole story is a *sham*."

"So, Will Davis doesn't work for them?"

"'Will Davis' may not even exist!" said Harry.

"In which case – who is he?"

"*Exactly*. And what's he up to in Mydworth?"

"More to the point – if he's a lie, what does that do to the case against Oliver?"

"Ah, see – well – as of now, not much," said Harry. "We've got no evidence to link him to the murder."

"Or even a motive."

"True," said Harry. "But at least – with this news – we have an angle of attack – something to dig our teeth into."

Kat looked away for a moment.

"Harry – we need to get into Davis's lodgings – find out who the hell he really is."

Before Harry could answer, Kat heard Maggie coming in at the kitchen door.

"*Cooee*," she called. "Only me."

"Maggie," called back Harry. "Perfect timing. Pop in, could you?"

Kat looked at him and he winked.

"Had an idea," he said to her.

What's he up to, she thought, as Maggie appeared at the door in her coat.

"More teas? Coffee?"

"Oh, we're fine, thanks," said Harry, "But we do have a question for you."

"Oh yes?"

"Do you fancy a little *espionage* this morning?"

"Espionage? *Spying*, you mean?" she said. "Well, that depends. Oh, wait…" Maggie leaned in conspiratorially. "This to do with young Oliver Brown?"

"It is," said Harry.

"Well then – what are you waiting for?" said the housekeeper. "Where do I sign up?"

HARRY PEERED IN through the window of the Green Man and could just see the landlord, Charlie, at one of the tables doing the morning's paperwork. Harry had known Charlie since the genial old publican had let him sit in the pub garden as a child, sipping free fizzy orange.

He tapped on the glass, and Charlie looked up, recognised him, and came to the doors to unlock.

"Sir Harry – unexpected pleasure," he said, opening the door and shaking Harry's hand. "Bit early for a snifter, old boy?"

"How are you, Charlie?" said Harry. "Mind if I bother you for a moment? Could use your help."

"Course. I'll get one of my boys to rustle up some coffees; we can go through to the snug, there's a fire already lit."

Harry followed him through the lounge bar to the cosy, private room at the back where he and Kat sometimes enjoyed a drink with local friends.

The Green Man prided itself on being the classiest of Mydworth's drinking holes, of which there were not a few.

"So, then, what can I do for you?" said Charlie.

"Two things," said Harry. "Want to talk to you about Ben Carmody and Mabel Brown."

"*I see.*"

Bit of caution there, Harry detected.

"And also a chap I noticed in here last night. Will Davis. Name ring a bell?"

"Will? That fella courting Connie Price?"

"That's the one," said Harry. C*ourting?* he thought.

S*o Will Davis's relationship with the housekeeper at Blackmead Farm is serious?*

Question was, why had neither of them mentioned it?

"Tell you what, Sir Harry – let me get that coffee organised," said Charlie, "and you can explain exactly what this is all about."

Harry got out his notebook, already jotting down more questions he needed to ask.

KAT SAT ON a hard wooden chair in the scullery of the Brown house while Mabel Brown settled little Elsie into a playpen dotted with toys.

She shivered slightly, even in her coat: the meagre fire burning in the stove didn't raise the temperature much more than outside. But the mug of tea that Mabel had just handed to her at least warmed her hands.

She watched Mabel at last come over to the scrubbed pine kitchen table and sit facing her. The woman's face so tired and strained; dark patches under her eyes.

"My Elsie… she won't settle for long," said Mabel, with a glance across at her daughter. "It's almost like she knows, you know? What's happening."

"I'm so sorry," said Kat. "This has to be so hard for you both."

Mabel didn't answer, then her eyes narrowed. The look stern, severe.

Terribly disappointed.

"You haven't found anything, have you?" she said, her voice low. "I can see it. You *can't* save my husband. That's why you've come here, isn't it? To tell me the worst."

Kat didn't want to raise the woman's hopes. But she knew she'd get nothing if she offered nothing.

"I'll be honest with you, Mabel. Until this morning, we *didn't* have anything. But something's come up that, well, doesn't make sense. Something that might be relevant – but we don't know how, or whether it really *is* important."

"What? I don't understand," said Mabel, her voice trembling. "You mean Oliver's going to go free?"

Kat quickly reached across and took Mabel's hand on the table:

"We don't *know*. Not yet. I can't offer you that hope. But I've got some questions for you. And what you tell me might help Ollie. Is that okay?"

In truth, Kat wasn't sure what Mabel might know about the mysterious Will Davis. But it was possible Oliver had talked about him. After all, Ollie, Ben and Will were supposedly "best mates".

She watched Mabel closely. The woman seemed to be wrestling with the decision. Then she looked round at Elsie, as if to check the little girl wasn't listening, and turned back to Kat.

"This is about the Green Man, isn't it?" she said.

Kat concealed her surprise. *What on earth was Mabel talking about? Did she know about Will and Connie last night?*

She nodded, waiting, wondering.

"That's what you want to know all about, isn't it?" continued Mabel.

Kat nodded again, hardly daring to breathe, not wanting to stop Mabel talking.

"I know I lied. Lied in the court. Lied to Ollie. I feel terrible about that."

Kat suddenly realised – Mabel was talking about her rumoured assignation with Ben Carmody.

"But, you see, I *had* to lie," continued Mabel. "I didn't want Ollie to think there *was* something going on with me and Ben. And then once I'd lied, I couldn't take it back."

"And the truth?" said Kat.

"Me and Ben wasn't seeing each other, I swear on her life," said Mabel, glancing across at her daughter. "But we *did* meet at the Green Man. Just once."

"Why?" said Kat, knowing there was no time to dance around the subject.

"I wanted to get to the bottom of all them ugly rumours – about me and him. Wanted to see if it was Ben himself that was spreading them."

"And was it?"

"No. He was in the dark like I was. Said it was just gossip. Told me to ignore it."

"But you couldn't, could you?" said Kat.

"*I* could – but Ollie couldn't. It was fair driving him mad! Trouble is – that night at the Green Man, someone saw us."

I bet I know who that was, thought Kat. *Will Davis…*

90

"And word got to Ollie. And I made the mistake of denying it, but Ollie didn't believe me and he lost it. And th-that's why he's going to die tomorrow."

Not if I can help it, thought Kat.

13.

A LITTLE MORE DIGGING

HARRY TOOK ANOTHER sip of his coffee then glanced up at the clock on the bar behind Charlie. Eleven o'clock.

Just twenty hours to the hanging, the time ticking away…

The landlord hadn't been very useful to begin with. He had no recollection of ever seeing Ben Carmody in the Green Man. Though, as he said, *"I don't work every shift, old boy, and, unless he was a regular, I could easily have missed him."*

But now the subject had moved onto Will Davis – and Harry was learning a *lot*.

"I first noticed him in July, I reckon," said Charlie. "Always takes a stool at the bar, very 'hail fellow well met', cheery sort of chap."

"Popular then?"

"With the locals? Yes – affable, friendly – generous! And with my barmen too – he always buys 'em a drink, always chatting away with 'em."

"Never any trouble?"

"Never. But you know what, Harry? Always felt something not quite *right* about him."

"In what way?" said Harry, knowing that Charlie's instincts were always spot on.

"Can't put my finger on it," said Charlie. "Cheerful chap he is, always lending people a helping hand if they need one, giving advice, buying his round."

"But?" said Harry, watching Charlie shaking his head.

"Only way I can describe it, it's like his face is all smiles, but behind those eyes it's as if… as if he's… somewhere else. Like he's calculating."

"Cold?"

"There you go! That's it. One time, I was behind the bar there, back to the punters, cleaning some glasses. In the mirror, I could see old Joseph Potter, one of my regulars, having a proper heart-to-heart with Davis. No idea about what. But then Joseph pops out to the privy out back, and soon as he's gone, Davis whips out this little notebook starts writing in it, quickly too. Then the minute Joseph comes back, Davis's slipped the notebook away, smooth as silk, like he was hiding the bloody crown jewels."

"A tad devious, you think?" said Harry, already wondering what might be in that notebook and how to get his hands on it.

"*Devious*, yes. Exactly. That's the word. Devious. Someone with something to hide!"

"When did Connie Price appear on the scene?" said Harry.

"Didn't take him long. Couple of months after he first turned up here, maybe. Quite a surprise that was, I must admit."

"Surprise? How so?"

"Sorry to say this, but, bit of an unlikely couple, if I'm honest. Sweet woman, she is, no doubt about that. But life's been pretty hard on her. One of the left-behinds, they call 'em, don't they? No love to be found. All them suitable fellas lost in the World War."

"Davis not her type, you think?"

"Don't get me wrong, Harry. Takes all sorts. But Davis: he's younger, educated and – like you said – slick. And well enough off, I'd say. But Connie – well I know she *says* she's the housekeeper, but seems to me she's still not more than a parlour maid. It just doesn't – to me – fit at all!"

Harry nodded. These old ideas of what constituted a "suitable partner" were taking forever to shift, it seemed.

Wonder what he must think of me and my American wife? Harry thought.

"They come in here together a lot?" he said.

"Every Wednesday, like clockwork. Always the same table, that one right over there in the corner, tucked away. Same drinks order, lots of cosy chats, hand-holding."

Harry looked across at that table now, and knew immediately that if he had a clandestine meeting in this pub, that would be the precise table he'd choose: it gave a view to all the entrances, but was dimly lit and would be barely noticeable to the other drinkers at the bar or the tables.

What was Davis up to? Could he really be attracted to Connie Price? Everything Charlie had told him so far suggested otherwise.

But then – what was his game?

"Oh, Sir Harry – that's your Maggie, isn't it?" said Charlie, gesturing up at the window behind him. "What *is* she doing?"

Harry looked around, and there, leaning against the window outside, was Maggie, pretending to read a newspaper.

"Ha, she's waiting for me, I do believe," said Harry, standing up and tapping on the window to attract her attention.

"She looks like one of them private detectives you read about."

"I'll tell her that," said Harry, buttoning up his coat. "Think she'll be flattered. Charlie, thanks for the coffee and the chat by the way. I owe you."

"No, you don't, Sir Harry," said Charlie. "This is all about Oliver Brown, isn't it?"

"It is."

"Well, I hope I've helped in some way. Though for the life of me I don't know how."

"Nor do I – yet," said Harry.

And he slipped out of the pub and round to the window where Maggie was waiting in softly falling snow.

"SHOULD WE BE seen together?" said Maggie, as he stepped close. "I mean, spies have to be careful, don't they?"

"Oh, I think we're safe enough out here," said Harry, smiling. Enjoying just how much Maggie was relishing her new role. "So then, what can you tell me?"

"Your Mr Davis? He left his lodgings just twenty minutes ago. And Mrs Pinder – by the way did you know her brother's married to my cousin from Winchester? – anyway, Mrs Pinder said he told her she could do his room and he won't be back until this evening."

"You're a marvel, Maggie, a true marvel."

"Oh, and that's not all," said Maggie, reaching into her handbag and taking out a key-ring. "Front door – and Mr Davis's door. To be handed back to me when you're done."

Harry took the keys and grinned.

THE WRONG MAN

"Seriously? I may have to recommend you to my superiors in London. Always on the hunt for a new recruit!"

"Just doing my bit," said Maggie, smiling, but then suddenly serious. "I only hope it helps."

"Me too," said Harry, then with a tip of his hat, he turned and headed off to Mrs Pinder's Board and Lodgings.

KAT TOOK A sip of tea from what she imagined was the guest teacup, and waited while Mabel put little Elsie down for a nap in the little truckle bed in the corner.

"Mabel, what do you know about Will Davis?" she said, when Mabel finally joined her again at the table.

"Will? Ollie's drinking buddy?"

Kat nodded.

"Seems *all right*," said Mabel. "I've only met him a couple of times. Ollie likes him. Says he's a good pal."

"He even tried to give Ollie an alibi, didn't he?" said Kat.

"I know. Think he wasn't very good at lying, though. Police saw through it straight away."

"Ollie and Will go back a long way, do they?" said Kat, persisting.

"No. Just a few months, that's all."

Kat could sense that Mabel was wearying of all these questions.

I'm not going to learn anything new here, she thought.

"Friend of Ben's too?"

"Was he?" said Mabel. "Could be. What men get up to in the pub, who they drink with, not for me to know."

"You never met up with Will?" said Kat, trying one last line of questions. "Maybe with Connie Price?"

"Connie? Why Connie?"

"She's Will Davis's sweetheart."

"Little Connie – and Mr Davis?" said Mabel, shaking her head. "Sorry. I can't believe that."

"You know her?"

"Known her for *years*," said Mabel. "Going back to when Ollie worked at Blackmead Farm."

Kat drew a breath. *What?*

This was something out of the blue…

"Wait. Ollie worked at the farm – with Ben?"

"Course. That's how I got to know Ollie," said Mabel. "I used to help out in the dairy sometimes. Ollie worked with the herd, for years, he did."

Kat saw Mabel get up, go to a shelf and bring over a small framed photograph showing three young people sitting on a hayrick.

"See, that's Ollie, Ben and Connie," said Mabel. "And that's me, by the side. Good ten years ago that must have been. First harvest after the war."

Kat tried to realign the facts to fit this new information: Ben, Ollie, Connie, Will – everything leading back to Blackmead Farm.

But why?

"Old Jeremiah… I tell you, he was the best thing ever happened to my Ollie," said Mabel, her face for a moment lifted, brighter. "Like a dad, he was. Fact – he always said when he passed away he'd see my Ollie right. And Ben too."

"How do you mean?"

"Jeremiah had no family," said Mabel. "Ollie took it to mean he'd maybe get left a bit in the old man's will."

"Could be a lot of money?" said Kat, thinking maybe there was a hint of a motive here.

"Once upon a time, maybe," said Mabel. "But all Jeremiah's going to leave is debts, from what I hear. Stony broke he is. Sad, isn't it?"

Then Mabel looked away. "Won't make much difference to Ollie, anyway, will it?"

Kat sat back. Seemed the inheritance wasn't a motive after all. But she made a mental note to talk to Harry about the old man's will. *Maybe there might be a way of checking?*

She heard Elsie start to cry and looked over. The little girl was stirring. Mabel got up to comfort her.

"I should be getting on too," said Kat, standing. Thanks so much for answering all those questions, Mabel."

"Don't know if they'll help," said Mabel, picking up Elsie and holding her tight in her arms. "Don't know if anything can help now."

Kat nodded. She knew there was nothing more she could say that wouldn't just sound like an empty platitude.

But she did at least have some new leads. And until they were followed up, she wasn't ready to give up hope on saving Oliver Brown from the gallows.

14.

SECRETS

COAT TIGHT AGAINST new falling snow, Harry climbed the steps of number 14 Crab Tree Lane, the set of keys that Maggie gave him in his gloved hand.

The house – respectable, in good order, prim and proper – stood in the middle of a terrace in a quiet part of Mydworth. The front window net-curtained, a small sign hanging: *temporary/permanent lodgings for gentlemen, enquire within*.

As he reached the top of the steps, he saw the curtain twitch to one side and a woman's face appear: Mrs Pinder, he assumed.

He smiled. The woman nodded back at him and the curtain twitched back.

Permission granted, thought Harry and he brushed the snow from his coat, opened the front door with the key and went in. Inside, the house smelt of polish and mothballs.

The key in his hand said "room 6", and Maggie had told him it was on the top floor. He started to climb the stairs, the carpet clean but thin under his boots.

On the landing, he spied a small cupboard and opened it. *Perfect.*

He took off his coat, hung it on a hook inside the door. Then he removed his boots, placed them in the cupboard too.

Don't want to leave tell-tale patches of melt-water in Davis's room.

He closed the cupboard door, then, in his socks, took the next flight of stairs. At each turn of the stairs there were a pair of numbered doors, until he reached the top – *room 6.*

He tapped on the door. Just in case there'd been a mix-up and Davis was actually at home. But no answer.

So, in he went, shutting the door quietly behind him.

He looked around. The room was barely furnished: bed, chest of drawers, wardrobe, desk and chair. One small armchair.

He checked his watch. The hours ticking away.

Then he started his search.

TEN MINUTES LATER, Harry went over to the armchair and sat, slowly – carefully – scanning the room.

The search had revealed... nothing.

In the chest – clothes neatly folded. In the wardrobe – two suits, weekend jacket and trousers. On the top of the wardrobe – an empty, good quality suitcase. By the bed – a bible.

On the desk – pen, papers, writing paper with the Consolidated letter-heading, envelopes, a blotter. *Interesting,* thought Harry. *Wonder how he got that?*

And in the desk drawer – some coins, paper clips, a pencil sharpener, a small screwdriver.

In short – absolutely nothing personal, or of value.

All of which still had Harry excited. Very excited indeed.

Because this was clearly the room of a man with secrets to hide.

Question was – where had he hidden them?

Over ten years of working with Intelligence – at first with the military, after the World War, then with the cover of diplomatic service in various British Embassies around the world – Harry had encountered many such spartan rooms. And all with many ingenious methods of hiding secrets.

It was possible, of course, that Davis's secrets were hidden in his car. But Harry couldn't shake the idea that Davis must have concealed his personal effects somewhere in this dull, bare room.

He scanned the ceiling. Not a mark on it. The ceiling rose dusty, and untouched. Then the walls: only one picture – and there could be no safe behind it, not here in temporary lodgings, for sure.

Which left the floor.

Brown, bare linoleum, with a large, threadbare rug in the centre of the room. He rolled up the rug: the aged linoleum was intact beneath it.

Now he got down on his hands and knees. Nothing under the bed – and nor did the flooring by the bed legs look marked or scraped.

The same with the floor under the wardrobe. But that was unlikely anyway – the big piece of furniture too heavy to move in a hurry, if required. And the desk – well that was too *easy* to move.

Which only left the chest of drawers. Harry ran his fingers over the linoleum in front of the piece of furniture.

And felt something.

At each side, there were slight indentations in the floor covering: the furniture had clearly been moved – enough times to have left the tell-tale marks.

He stood up, slid the chest of drawers into the centre of the room, then got down on his knees again to examine the exposed flooring. To see… that a small section of lino had been carefully sliced open, then tacked back into place with the smallest of flat-headed nails.

He got up, went to the desk drawer, took out the screwdriver, then knelt by the nails, and levered them out.

As expected, the screwdriver was the perfect tool, popping the nails out quickly.

Then he gently peeled back the lino: underneath he saw floorboards. But more importantly, a small section of the timber floor – barely a foot long – that he could see had been recently cut.

Easy enough to do with the right saw, thought Harry. *Just pick an afternoon when the house was empty.*

He inserted the screwdriver (again – the perfect tool) and levered the piece of wood out to see…

A metal box, maybe a foot square.

He lifted the box out, taking care not to leave any marks, then went over to the desk, put the box down and opened the lid.

The box was crammed tight. Piece by piece, Harry took out the contents, lining them up on the desk so he would know exactly how to replace them. The idea being – that Davis would never suspect he'd had a visitor.

But when Harry saw some of the contents of the box, he knew he couldn't take the risk of leaving it here for Davis to destroy on his return.

Because this was more than just secrets: this looked to Harry like *evidence*.

KAT FINISHED THE last morsel of cheese and cucumber sandwich and pushed her plate to one side.

"The tension is killing me, Harry," she said, staring at the metal box which sat between them on the kitchen table of the Dower House.

Harry had insisted on them both grabbing some late lunch – even though time was running out, he'd said they had to eat. *"If we're right about this,"* he'd said, *"we've got a long day, and maybe night, ahead of us."*

Maggie had made up a stack of sandwiches and a big pot of tea, while she and Harry caught up with what they had each learned.

The metal box though, could only be properly inspected when they were wearing gloves. Removing it from its hiding place might have weakened its strength as evidence, but there would be no doubt about fingerprints – and she and Harry both doubted Davis had worn gloves every time he'd opened it.

So now, gloves on, she waited as Harry reached across and opened the lid of the box.

"Soon as I saw these," said Harry, lifting out some wooden stamps and a print pad and ink, "I knew we were dealing with a pro."

Kat examined the stamps: each one bearing the name of a different insurance company.

"So Consolidated isn't the *only* insurance scam our Mr Davis has worked," she said.

"Not just insurance," said Harry. "Some of these rubber stamps are government issue. But look at the rest of this stuff."

Harry took out jewellery boxes, opened them. Kat saw rings, necklaces, bracelets, brooches. She picked one up.

"Gold. Diamonds. Rubies. This lot must be worth hundreds of pounds."

"I'll say. Look at this one," said Harry, showing her a ring with an elaborate crest.

She could see the name "Urquhart".

"This must be Jeremiah's signet ring," she said.

"I'm thinking, if he and Connie are courting, it's very likely he's been a regular visitor to Blackmead Farm," said Harry. "Lots of opportunities to pilfer whatever treasures old Jeremiah had left."

"And maybe, somehow, he got on the wrong side of Ben?" said Kat.

"Or felt that Ben was onto him," said Harry. "Hence, Ben had to go. Bit of a motive there?"

Kat reached into the box and started carefully pulling out objects herself.

"Hey. Look at this," she said. "A roll of US dollars."

She saw Harry place a pile of letters on the table next to them. "Love letters – from Connie." Then he placed a pill box on the table. She picked it up – and read the label: "Luminal. Sleeping tablets, yes?"

"Yes. Powerful ones, at that," said Harry. "Either Davis has a problem sleeping, or—"

"He uses them to put people out," said Kat. "Wait – remember Ollie said he couldn't remember what happened, you know, after he left the pub?"

"You're right. Like he was drugged," said Harry. "But there's more. Look at the label. It's a prescription from a pharmacy in Manchester – to a Mr William Pace. Not Davis – but close."

"So, he uses different identities – maybe always keeping the name Will."

"Makes sense," said Harry, sitting back now the box was empty. "Question is – what do we do now? And how does any of this tie into the murder of Ben Carmody?"

"Well, we know Davis is a con artist and thief. If he's also a murderer – perhaps this isn't the first time?"

"The job done on Ben Carmody… not the work of a first-timer I'd say. So, if we can find out who the hell he is – and if he's got a violent background – it just might be enough for a judge to grant Ollie a stay of execution."

"That's a mighty 'if' though, Harry. And without a motive for killing Ben, there's nothing to build a case on."

"And then there's the damn time… running out!"

Kat looked up at the clock on the kitchen wall. Four o'clock – and already getting dark outside.

The execution at dawn tomorrow…

"We have to find out who Davis really is," she said. "What if we go to Timms? There's enough evidence here, surely, to have him arrested?"

"There is. But once we set those wheels in motion, they run slowly, Kat. Too slowly to save Ollie."

"You're right."

"But we do need access to police records so we can see if there's a match somewhere with Davis's MO," said Harry. "Enough to give us his real identity."

"I can't see Timms giving us that kind of access," said Kat.

Then she had a thought. "But you know – there *is* somebody who might."

15.

THE LONG ARM OF THE LAW

HARRY SAT IN the back office of Mydworth Police Station, listening as Kat explained the situation to young Constable Loxley – Timms fortuitously out on a case.

On the table between them – the tin box, its contents laid out. The rings, jewellery, cash, letters.

"So then, you want me to arrest this Davis character?" said Loxley, sitting back, arms folded.

"Right," said Kat. "We know he has stolen things from Jeremiah Urquhart. Once in custody, we might be able to find out who he is. And if he killed Ben Carmody."

"It's a big 'if'," said Loxley. "You suggest Carmody might have uncovered Davis's stealing – but apart from that, you don't have a motive."

Harry saw Kat nod at that, choosing her next words carefully.

"We don't. And we don't have any time either. But unless we investigate Davis, his past, his possible guilt, before dawn tomorrow—"

Loxley finished the thought: "An innocent man will have been hanged?"

Harry saw Kat nod at that. For a few moments, silence. Then:

"Okay," said Loxley, pushing his chair back and standing. "I'll have my head handed to me on a plate, that's for sure. But let's go find Davis."

HARRY HAD BARELY reached the top of the stone steps, before Mrs Pinder had the front door of the lodging house open.

No need for a key this time, not with a police car outside and a constable by his side.

He let Loxley explain.

"Mrs Pinder, I'm here to see your lodger, William Davis, on a very serious police—"

"Oh – come on in," said Mrs Pinder, shaking her head. "But, I'll tell you now, he's *not* here. Not half an hour ago, came flying right in here, he did! Running up to his room. Made a terrible racket up there. Shouts! Curses! Words I can't repeat. Proper temper on him!"

Harry felt Kat shoot him a look, the reason for Davis's quick departure clear.

"Mind if we take a look?" Harry said.

"Be my guest."

And Harry started up the stairs, Kat by his side.

He wondered if she felt the way he did: that Davis had just outplayed them.

And was now gone.

"And another thing," the old woman said from the bottom of the stairs, "he had his bags. All packed, he was."

Leaving Harry with the thought: *I know exactly what we're about to find in Davis's room.*

KAT QUICKLY TOOK in the obvious as they entered and flicked on the electric light switch. The room, which Harry had described as "spartan" – now empty. The only thing of interest – the hidey-hole for the metal box.

The chest of drawers had been dragged away, that hole left open.

Davis had clearly come back here, alarmed by what she and Harry had been doing, the questions, the digging into things.

Had he spotted them watching him in the Green Man with his secret paramour, the unlikely Connie?

"Gone," Loxley said. "Done a runner. I'll get out an alert – nearby stations. Though Sergeant Timms will need to sign off on that."

Kat tried to guess Davis's train of thought coming back here.

First, realising that his fraud and thievery had been discovered. Then, arrest suddenly looming. And finally seeing his treasure trove, missing from its hiding place. Leaving Davis with…

Well, with what exactly?

All these months since Ben's death, Davis had stayed with Connie, still – in the parlance of a con man – "working" her. Taking her out for drinks at the Green Man; probably visiting her at the farm.

There had to be a reason. Something she and Harry had missed.

Kat knew there was only one place that "reason" might be hiding.

"We have to go to Blackmead Farm."

Harry turned to her, his face quizzical.

"What Davis was doing there, with Connie, the old man, that place – *can't* just be   about what we found in the tin box. And if he's leaving, his name to be abandoned, some new identity to be created… Then he has unfinished business at Blackmead."

She took a breath.

"Harry – we got to go now."

"I'd better come too," said Loxley. "If he's there—"

But Harry turned to the constable.

"Loxley, I rather think we must ask you to let us go *alone*…"

"But you have no authority, Sir Harry. And Davis could—"

Harry put up his hand. "I *know*. But if all we get this Davis character for is petty theft – and we miss whatever else he was doing – an innocent man will swing."

Loxley's eyes were fixed on Harry. Young, inexperienced, but, Kat knew, smart. And now, listening with all ears.

"There's an important job back at the station that only *you* can do, old chap," said Harry. "Starting with scouring the records for any crimes with the same MO as our con man Davis. False names, false jobs, the gaining of confidences, the stealing – and also, I suspect – the midnight flit. And more importantly – are there any other murders where the method matches that of Carmody? Murders where the killer escaped."

Kat added, "Whoever killed Carmody knew how to handle a knife. That was no random stabbing."

"Unsolved murders?" said Loxley. "You think Davis not only killed Carmody – but he's killed before?"

"Yes," said Kat. She knew they had to be going. Minutes counted here.

"Let us handle Davis," said Harry. "If he's there, we'll stop him."

"And if he is the killer?" Loxley said. "If he *is* dangerous?"

Kat turned to Harry.

"Wouldn't be the first time – for either of us," she said.

"All right," said Loxley, finally. "I'll do what I can – with or without Sergeant Timms' help."

"Good man," said Harry, a hand on the constable's shoulder.

And together they turned from the now empty room, and went fast down the dim stairs.

At the now-open front door, Mrs Pinder – shaken by all the activity – stood as if watching some terribly suspenseful play.

As Kat passed, she gave her a smile and a simple "thank you".

"If you find him," called the landlady after them, "you tell 'im he owes me a month's rent!"

16.

THE TRUTH ABOUT BLACKMEAD FARM

KAT GAVE HARRY directions as he hurled the Alvis through the snow-covered country lanes that led to Blackmead Farm, the car sliding then recovering, engine racing.

The snow had finally stopped falling, and, in the clearing night sky, a sharp moon cast harsh shadows across the frozen fields.

Finally, they slithered to a halt outside the front door, the big old building heavy with drifted snow, only a couple of lights visible within.

In the moonlight, she didn't see any sign of Davis's car – and there were no tell-tale tyre tracks in the snow either. Could they already be too late? But she knew he could easily have driven up one of the farm tracks, parked his Austin over by the abandoned barn, or even in the back.

"No telling what we're walking into here," Harry said, killing the engine and turning to her.

"We'll be careful then. As always."

And at that Harry smiled, "*As always.*"

Almost in unison, they popped open the car's doors, and hurried, bent double, through the swirling snow to the front door, hoping that their hunches had been right, and inside they'd find Will Davis.

INSIDE THE HOUSE, all sort of alarm bells went off in Kat's head. She had done some scary things in some very intimidating places, not knowing what lay ahead.

But this? Knowing what was at stake and what they might face, was right up there with the scariest of them.

The first thing she saw was Connie huddled against a hallway wall.

Crying loudly.

Has she been hit? Kat wondered.

All she had to say was: "Is he *here*?"

And Connie freed one arm and pointed up the stairs, lit so dimly by the meagre wall lights.

"What's up there?" said Harry.

"Jeremiah's rooms," said Kat. "The old man can't come down – he must be up there, now with Davis."

Kat saw Harry pause at the foot of the stairs.

"Go," she said. "Be right behind you. Want to make sure Connie here is okay."

Harry nodded, and she saw him take the stairs two at a time while she went to the sobbing woman.

Kat crouched down, looking to see if there was any wound, any sign of violence.

"Are you hurt?" she said.

"I'll live," said Connie, wiping her eyes and pushing herself back onto her feet. And then she uttered words that Kat had heard more than once from women who had been used: *"I'm such a fool."*

HARRY REACHED THE top of the stairs, and stopped. From down the dark hallway to his right he heard voices. One of them strong, forceful, demanding.

The other, *more like the croak of a wounded creature.*

Harry couldn't wait – not if Davis was in there with Urquhart. So, he ran straight down the hallway and into what he guessed must be the old man's room, to see something that sickened him.

The crumpled figure of an old man was sprawled on the floor – obviously having been dumped out of a chair – stranded on the faded carpet.

Jeremiah Urquhart.

Standing over him threateningly, his horn-rimmed glasses gone, clearly a prop, stood Will Davis.

In Davis's hand, another metal box; but this one small, ancient.

"Davis. What the hell—?"

Seeing Harry arrive, Davis acted in a surprising way. No sense of alarm or worry. Instead, an actual hint of a *smile.* Those eyes widening.

"*You.* Just couldn't let things go, could you? Only hours away, and—" he gestured at Urquhart using his foot, a kick to the man's side "—none of this would have happened. Well, you see, I could really use the key to this box. I mean, I already know what's in here. But the old man doesn't seem inclined to give it to me."

Another kick to Urquhart. Harry took a step.

But Urquhart had enough wind in his lungs to say: "Nothing in there. *Nothing.*"

Harry doubted that. But clearly, Will Davis – in his rooting around Urquhart's possessions – had found out what was there.

"Put the box down, Davis," he said.

Davis laughed.

"Ha! You know, I *have* got rather fond of that name. Will Davis! Quite the thoughtful character. But, as to your request…"

Harry watched – he had expected this – as Davis slid out his long folding knife, and, with one hand, flipped the blade open.

"… *I must decline,*" Davis said. "Or—"

As Harry stood there he reminded himself, if what they suspected was true, Davis knew how to use that knife. He moved slowly to the side, as if compliant with Davis's order.

Another smile and nod from the man holding the open knife.

"Who needs the damn key anyway," Davis said as he stepped over Urquhart's body, with the old man muttering into the carpet.

"You won't get away with this," said Harry.

To which Davis, his eyes on Harry with each careful step, said, "Oh, I think I *will.*"

Until Davis was nearly at the door – knife in one outstretched hand, box tucked under the other arm.

Where he got an unpleasant surprise.

For Harry could see something that Davis could not.

Kat.

Standing in the hallway, just outside the doorway.

And as Davis turned to make his getaway, he had no chance, as Kat sent her left forearm flying up against Davis's right hand holding the knife,   hitting it *hard*, just at the wrist,

114

and smacking his hand against the wooden doorframe with an audible *thwack*.

The knife went tumbling to the floor.

Harry raced to the door as well, Davis momentarily stunned, staggering backwards into the hallway.

KAT SAW THE knife fall as she knew it would, having learned that move years ago from an old city cop who came in to her father's bar.

Telling her: *"You never know, Kat. Someday you might need this."*

As it turned out, she'd used the move more than once in the years since.

And so far, it had never failed.

Now she watched Davis recover his balance, push off from the wall and take a step towards her, ready surely to charge her out of the way so he could reach the stairs behind her.

But then Harry appeared at her side – Davis's route to the stairs effectively blocked.

And for a second Kat thought – *we've got him.*

But then Davis did something she didn't understand.

He turned, and ran farther down the hallway, *away* from the stairs.

"Nice work with the knife," said Harry. "Wish I could have seen Davis's face."

"Quite the picture," said Kat.

"What's happened?" came Connie's voice from behind her.

Kat turned to see the housekeeper hurrying up the stairs.

"Mr Urquhart, is he—?"

"Connie – can you see to him?" said Harry. "He's been badly roughed up."

"Where's Davis gone?" said Connie, looking around anxiously. "Where is that monster?"

Kat pointed down the dim hallway, just catching sight of Davis at the other end, disappearing into... *well, what exactly?*

"Wait – is there another staircase along there?" said Harry, urgently. "Another way down?"

"No," said Connie. "That's the way *up*. To the attic. To the roof."

"The roof?" said Harry. "Oh well. I'd better, as they say, *give chase*."

To which Kat said simply, "You go. I'll head outside, see if I can see him. Cut him off if he tries to get down."

And leaving Connie to look after the old man, she took one quick last look at Harry and raced to the stairs.

17.

AN UNLIKELY EXIT

HARRY ENTERED THE attic, dust motes dancing in the scant moonlight that seeped in through smeared windows set into the sharply peaked roof.

He saw Davis at one of the windows at the far end, opening it.

And actually, climbing out.

"Davis," Harry said, "what the *hell* are you doing? Game's up."

But the words did nothing to slow Davis, and Harry guessed the man must know something about this attic that Harry didn't.

Harry dodged the boxes and dingy muslin cloths covering who knew what, to get to the window. The air shooting in, frigid, and the sill outside glistening with an icy sheen.

Harry leaned out. Davis had started navigating the sharply angled roof, one hand still grimly holding the metal box, the other digging into the tiles, as he crab-clawed away.

Which to Harry seemed like a completely insane idea – but then, in the cold moonlight he saw the top of a narrow metal ladder poking out of the snow at the end of the roof, and he understood Davis's plan.

A fire escape – probably leading down to where Davis had his car. The man clearly just minutes from a successful getaway.

Harry shook his head. The prospect of climbing out onto the roof... madness in the day, let alone at night. All of the tiles coated with ice that glistened treacherously. The frozen stonework probably so slick. And a terrifying fall to the ground three storeys below.

Despite his lack of enthusiasm (and tightened stomach muscles) he mumbled: "Well, in for a penny—"

And he climbed out.

HARRY FOLLOWED DAVIS'S path, who only looked back a couple of times, focused on securing his footholds.

At any other time, this clear, bright night would have been one to enjoy: Harry could see so many sparkling stars in the blackness above, and in the distance, across shimmering white fields, the slumbering town of Mydworth, the street gas lights giving it an orange glow.

But Harry wasn't here for the view. This was a deadly challenge. The slate roof – so icy, his feet slipped even as his fingers dug into the edge of the tiles.

Madness indeed, he thought. One false move, and he'd go sliding down to the frozen ground below.

He looked at Davis, who was halfway to the simple metal ladder. Below, Harry spied a car, the Austin that Davis had mentioned in the pub. Nothing flashy to catch anyone's attention.

He wondered if Kat had figured out the escape route. If Davis got to that ladder before them, he'd be in the car in seconds, then *away*.

But Harry knew the danger of hurrying, and forced himself to make sure that each foothold and handhold was as secure as possible, even at the cost of closing the distance between him and Will Davis.

Then he spotted a gap in the roof just ahead where the tiles had chipped and broken away entirely, revealing exposed wood. It was a place where – with a big step – he could get closer to the fleeing Davis, who still was amazingly using only one hand to make his getaway.

Harry edged towards that bare spot, feeling the sole of his shoe connect with the rough edge where bare wood met the still intact stone tiles surrounding it. His eyes scanned the darkness – if he could just grab a stone tile, and it held, he should be able to slide over...

So, he thought, *here goes.*

AMAZINGLY, HE MANAGED to slide over the jagged gap, as if somehow his *imagining* the manoeuvre was enough information for his body to then *carry it out.*

This time, he thought.

Davis was now a few yards closer. But so was the ladder.

He saw Davis start to do his own next slide over. One that would put the top curved bars of the ladder easily within striking distance.

Davis moved.

And then Harry heard a *crack.* The stone tile Davis had grabbed split in *two,* pieces flying away, and all Harry could do was watch as Davis began a terrible slide down the sharply sloped roof.

For a second, Davis's feet seemed to catch some kind of protrusion, momentarily slowing him.

But then *those* tiles gave way too, and Davis slid to the very edge of the roof, his legs suddenly dangling in space.

One hand locked on a last tile, somehow miraculously holding him in place. But the situation – hopeless. Harry only feet away, knowing the life of Oliver Brown depended on keeping Will Davis alive.

And instead of continuing to the ladder and escaping this crazily dangerous rooftop, Harry started lowering himself down to the fleeing man.

"DAVIS. LET THE damn box *go*. And here – grab my hand, man. Before it's too late."

Harry extended his hand down, inches away from Davis's left hand which was still locked onto the metal box.

"*Drop the box*. Take my hand. Let's get off this damn roof!"

Then Davis looked up.

And Harry could see the answer in the man's wild eyes even before the slightest of head shakes – *no*.

Harry's hand still extended – but in a moment, all that became useless as Davis's fingers gave up the impossible challenge.

And Harry watched the man slip over the side of the house.

For a second, all Harry did was watch Davis fall into space.

But then, down below, he saw another figure standing in the deep snow at the back of the house.

Kat.

Harry let himself watch Davis's terrible landing, just feet from his wife, and only then – knowing a similar fate awaited him with a single misstep – started towards the ladder again, even more slowly.

Wondering: *Is Davis dead?*

And, if so, just how much that would hurt their chances of ever finding out the answer to the one question that would save Oliver Brown's life.

Was Will Davis the killer?

18.

A LONG NIGHT

KAT WATCHED DAVIS land in the snow, on his side, and for a moment the man didn't move, and she feared the worst.

But then Davis looked up, moaned, and raised his head.

Alive.

Saved by the deep snow.

She walked over to him and picked up the small metal box which had fallen in the snow by his side.

"We'll get you some help, Davis. Back in Mydworth." Then to make things perfectly clear. "Back at the *jail*. But think we'd best wait until Sir Harry gets down here, eh?"

In Davis's eyes, Kat saw something that was – even now, with the man crumpled before her – chilling. A look in those eyes that seemed to say only one thing: *I'd kill you if I could.*

Kat looked over to the old fire escape ladder that ran from the ground to the rooftop.

As Harry hit the ground and raced over.

"Ah, still alive," he said, peering down at Davis. "Well, *that's* rather amazing. Saved by the snow, I imagine."

She went to him. "Harry, you okay?"

"Me? Bit chilled. Fingers a little achy, you know. Otherwise, never better."

She saw him look up at the rooftop. "Though I think I shall avoid any roof climbing in the near future."

Then, she watched him   lean down.

"Mr Davis, it turns out you are one *very lucky* fellow. Now, if you don't mind waiting here just a few more minutes I'll see if I can rustle up some rope. Tie you up, just to be sure? Won't be a moment."

Harry stood up and looked at his watch.

"I know," Kat said. "Time running out."

And Harry nodded as he hurried back into Blackmead Farm.

Kat turned back to look at Davis, now propped up on one arm.

"I say, Lady Mortimer," he said, his voice wheezy. "Help me up, would you? Leg's killing me."

"I *think* – no. Sorry."

"Please – I'm begging you," he said, pushing himself up further, wincing from the pain. "I mean – come on. Arm's broken for sure, leg's shot – I'm hardly going to run, now, am I?"

Kat looked at his pleading face, his eyes so sincere.

So deceptive.

"Guess you're used to fooling people, right Davis? Not this time, I'm afraid."

She watched him sink back onto his uninjured arm. And now it was clear to him that she wasn't intending to help – that open, charming face darkened, as if a switch had been turned. The eyes suddenly empty.

"By the way," he said. "Now it's just the two of us – you must tell me how you did it."

"Did what?"

"Oh – you know – snared Sir Harry there? Quite the catch—"

"What are you talking about?"

"Have to give it to you. Common girl from the Bronx, no money – no proper vowels even – snags a proper English lord of the manor, still with money to his name? Why, I imagine when the dear old aunty pegs it there'll be a few million coming your way, eh?"

His grin turned even more *slimy*.

"Well played… *Yank*."

Kat couldn't quite believe this garbage Davis was spouting. In a flash, she felt angry.

But she didn't rise to it. *That would be exactly what he wanted…*

Instead, she played along.

"I don't know what you mean."

"Oh, *really*? I must say – I'm full of admiration. One hell of a line you must have thrown him – and he took the bait, hook, line and sinker." Then, as if the taunts could go even lower… "I'm guessing you might have some other… *talents*… as well."

Kat took a quiet breath. *Steady*, she thought. And then it was her turn.

"You mean – same way you snagged Connie?" said Kat with a shrug, using his own words back on him.

"Connie? That one? Oh, she was *so* easy. Sweet little thing, but hardly the best goods left on the shelf. 'On the shelf', being the operative words, of course."

Kat wished Davis was – in fact – standing. *Would be so gratifying to punch him hard in the gut.*

"Guess she must have been grateful when you showed an interest?"

"What do you think? Couldn't believe her bloody luck. Good looking, thoughtful chap like 'Will Davis'."

"Right. But not sure I follow. What I don't get is why," said Kat. "Why *her*?"

"Ha! Nice try. I'm not going to tell you that."

124

"You played her, though, didn't you? Must be a really good reason."

"Everybody plays everybody. You of all people must know that – *Kat Reilly*."

Kat smiled, hiding how she really felt about this lowlife.

"I imagine that Connie wasn't the first?" she said.

"Of course not. Takes time—"at this he tapped his skull "—to acquire the necessary skills. Though I was rather hoping she'd be the last."

What did that mean? thought Kat. *What was so special about Connie Price?*

She saw him glance across at the farm, perhaps realising he was running out of time.

"Come on, let me up," he said, smiling again, turning on the charm. "What harm can it do?" Then a tease: "Maybe I'll tell you more about why poor, drab Connie Price…"

But before she could answer, Harry emerged from the farmhouse, carrying a coil of rope.

"All right," said Harry as he approached. "Afraid you'll be tied up for a while, Davis."

"Damn you," said Davis, his voice now harsh again, staring straight into Kat, his game about to fail. A man so used to tricking and trapping women.

Not this time…

"This rotter cause you any trouble, Lady Mortimer?" said Harry, coming near.

"Him? *Not a bit,*" said Kat, not wanting to repeat the conversation. "Let's get him tied up, nice and *tight*, and then…" she grinned at this, looking right at Davis "…throw him into the car."

THE WRONG MAN

KAT STOOD BESIDE Harry near Sergeant Timms' desk, Constable Loxley off to one side, while Timms passed them a sheaf of papers.

The doctor was still with Davis, tending to him in his cell. The worst of his injuries as it turned out, no more than a broken arm.

"Loxley here, um, has done some good work, Sir Harry, Lady Mortimer. These crime reports are just the open Sussex investigations – fraud, extortion, larceny – got Mr Davis's fingerprints all over them if I'm not mistaken."

"The notebook?" Harry said, as if reminding Timms of something overlooked.

"Ah, yes. Right. That does seem to confirm just about all of them, names, dates, places. Yup, so very little doubt. All good for the county clear-up rate, no doubt about that!"

Kat looked up at the big Genalux clock on the wall, the second hand ticking onwards...

2am. Just six hours until dawn.

And Timms seeming to have missed the bigger picture – the imminent execution. She looked across at Loxley who took his cue and cleared his throat.

"Sergeant," he said. "The other matter?"

Timms looked up to his new constable, no sign of pleasure at whatever Loxley was reminding him about.

"Oh, yes. Sir Harry, er, I gather you asked my constable to make some... *telephone calls*... to other county police forces?"

"I did, sergeant," said Harry. "You were unavailable, you see. It's our belief that Davis may be responsible for Ben Carmody's death, and if that's true, it's highly likely he has killed before. Using the same methods."

Kat added: "And the same weapon."

"Yes, Constable Loxley told me your 'theory'."

Kat watched the portly policeman wrestle with this unorthodox situation, before finally settling on an answer.

"The constable has – so he tells me – found two cases of murder where the *modus operandi* seems to match what happened to poor Ben Carmody."

Kat couldn't hold back any longer.

"Then you can call Pentonville? Get the hanging postponed? At least—"

But Timms was already shaking his head.

"M'lady, I'm afraid we simply have nothing here that warrants interfering with the due process of justice. No evidence at *all* that Davis is a killer. Simply some coincidental – and unsolved – crimes."

Then Loxley – *Bless him, Kat thought* – turned to Harry and her and said a key word.

"*Yet.* One of the murders, sir… in Newcastle. There was a suspect who was arrested, but then somehow escaped custody."

"Arrested?" said Harry. "But that must mean they have a photograph."

"They do indeed, sir," said Loxley.

Kat looked to Harry, understanding the implication of this immediately.

"Hang on! If we can prove that Will Davis and this suspect are one and the same, surely that would be enough to warrant a stay of execution?" she said, looking to Timms.

"I can't be certain," Timms finally said with a shrug. "But I imagine… yes, it would."

She watched him sit back in his chair, take a sip from his mug of tea.

THE WRONG MAN

"But with just," a glance at the clock, "a few hours before the hanging, how are we to magic a photo of the suspect from Newcastle to Mydworth, may I ask?"

"Telephotography," said Loxley.

Kat spun round to look at him. In her last posting, the embassy had the newly invented device which miraculously could send pictures over the phone lines.

"Wait. You've got a machine here?" she said, scarcely able to believe it.

Timms cleared his throat.

"Well, yes. It was delivered a few months ago. Though, to be honest, we've not had a single reason to use it. Or to set the darned thing up."

"Till *now*," Loxley said, risking the wrathful glance of Timms again.

"Well, come on – what are we waiting for?" said Harry. "Be a feather in your cap, Timms, if you solve a murder using the very latest weapon in the police armoury, eh?"

Kat caught Harry's eye – trusting this flattery might work better with Timms than a kick in the—

And sure enough, Timms responded in fashion.

"Come on Loxley," said the sergeant. "You *heard* Sir Harry! Get that damn machine out of its crate – and start reading the bloody manual!"

As Loxley gave her a discreet smile and disappeared into the back office, Kat saw the doctor emerge from the cells with Constable Thomas.

"I've bandaged him up as best I can," said the doctor, taking his coat from the stand and putting it on. "But he'll need to have that arm properly set in the morning."

"Thank you, doctor," said Timms.

"Is he in a fit state to   talk?" said Harry.

128

The doctor grinned. "Oh, his mouth seems to be working just *fine*. Rather garrulous, actually. Yes, so medically there's no reason why not." The doctor snapped closed his medical bag. "By all means – have at him…"

The doctor left, and Kat looked at Harry.

While they were waiting for Loxley to get the machine running, the only hope of any other breakthrough was via Davis himself.

"All right with you if we have a little chat with our suspect?" said Harry to Timms.

Timms shrugged: "Help yourself. But I wouldn't raise your hopes, Sir Harry. I know that type. Too clever by half. He'll be all zipped up. Not a peep, I imagine, least with you two asking questions."

Kat got up and joined Harry as Constable Thomas unlocked the door to the cells.

She suspected – based on her chat with Davis earlier – that Timms might be right.

Davis wasn't going to give anything away.

Which meant everything rested on Loxley and the Telephotography machine.

And time was running out…

19.

THE FINAL HOURS

AN HOUR LATER, and Kat emerged from the cells, none the wiser, Harry beside her, shaking his head.

Sure, Davis had listened politely to each question – and then declined to answer. And all the time, as Kat had sat opposite him, he had held a half-smile on her, as if mocking their inability to get him to talk.

Kat looked around the main station room: Timms still sat by the fire, a mug of tea as ever by his side.

But now, on the desk, stood the Telephotography machine. The same size as the devices that she had herself used in the past, but this one, a newer model, shaped more like a radiogram.

Loxley stood to one side, screwing in a cable, and he looked up when she and Harry approached.

"How are you getting on?" said Kat.

No way to hide the hint of desperation in her question.

"Just fine-tuning it," said Loxley.

"And you think it will work?"

Loxley picked up a piece of paper, handed it to her.

"Tested it already," he said. "Called a pal in Fleet Street just now. Here – this is the front page of tomorrow's *Times*."

Loxley handed Harry some pages.

"I say," said Harry. "Extraordinary."

"What about Newcastle?" said Kat. "They all set to send?"

"They *were*," said Loxley. "But now they've got a problem with their damned machine."

Kat fired a look at Harry. To be *this* close. And more minutes ticking away.

"Oh no."

"They're trying to locate another. But with this same weather up north – not so easy."

Kat nodded, then said the obvious…

"So, all we can do is wait and hope they manage it."

And Harry added solemnly: "*All before dawn.*"

To which Timms replied.

"I'm afraid so."

Kat looked up at the clock again. Nearly four.

Constable Thomas appeared from the kitchen, making himself useful by bearing a tray with mugs of tea and a plate of biscuits.

She took one eagerly, realising that neither she nor Harry had eaten since lunch the day before.

As she put down her plate, she saw the metal box that Davis had taken from Blackmead Farm, the lid now open, the box overflowing with papers.

"I forgot to ask – what was in there?" she said.

"Old receipts, invoices, mostly," said Timms. "Last century, would you believe. American, some of it."

Kat walked over to the table, and began to shuffle through the contents of the box, the papers dry and dusty, as if untouched for years.

"Funny thing for Davis to want to steal," continued Timms. "All looks pretty worthless to me."

Kat took out a roll of papers, tied with legal tape, slid the papers out and opened them up gently, careful not to tear them.

And for a second – she couldn't quite believe what she was reading...

Standard Oil Stock issue, 1838...

"Harry," she said. "Look."

And Harry came to join her, peering at the papers in her hand.

"What is it?"

"If I'm not mistaken," said Kat, "it's a motive for murder."

And at that, even Timms stood up.

She opened the papers further, skimmed through the others.

"Jeremiah said he'd been to Texas, years ago, right?" she said. "But he *didn't* tell me he'd bought shares in oil. Standard Oil no less. Bought, then forgotten – or maybe he thought them worthless. But – if I'm not mistaken – these stock certificates, today? Must be worth a fortune."

"Too right. With the current oil boom in Texas? These could be worth more than blocks of gold. Davis must have found the papers while he was pilfering," said Harry. "But why get involved with Connie? Why not just con the old man? Steal the stock?"

Kat looked away for second. But then – it was *there*.

"I *know*. Because Connie's *in* Jeremiah's will. She gets a third of the estate."

"Sorry, Lady Mortimer. But exactly *how* is that a motive for murder?" said Timms, scratching his ample stomach.

"Ben Carmody and Oliver Brown are the other two beneficiaries," said Kat. "Two birds, one stone, don't you see? Davis kills Ben, and Oliver   hangs for the crime. Then as

132

Connie's spouse, he picks up all three shares of the inheritance in one go."

"And then disposes of Connie some time down the line…" said Harry.

"Well, that is certainly one nasty piece of work," said Timms, now clearly persuaded of Davis's guilt. "Question is – have we uncovered this all too late?"

Kat looked at Harry. The question devastating.

Had they come this far only – in the end – to fail?

As she looked up at the clock again, and its relentless ticking…

TIMMS SNORED AT his desk. Loxley kept circling the Telephotography machine.

Harry, more than once, walked over to her.

"How you doing here, Kat?"

"Well, *Sir Harry*. I've had a few late nights in my time. Things at stake and all. But one like this?"

She shook her head.

The clock on the wall had slowly ticked off the hours, and now it neared six.

"Thinking," Harry said, his face set, "that if it gets too late, they will stop looking for a machine till morning. Weather horrible up there, too."

"And I've been trying to *not* think that."

She saw Loxley look over. She realised that if Oliver Brown did go free, it would be due as much to Loxley as the two of them.

But with the minutes slipping away like the sands in an hour glass, that prospect seemed less and less likely.

More than once, amidst this waiting, Kat thought of Ollie's wife, Mabel, and his little girl. No sleep happening at that home she guessed…

Must be such torture, Kat thought.

Then there was the bulky Telephotography machine itself, silent, with a phone line snaking into it.

But it might as well be sleeping, just like the sergeant himself.

And Kat said: "I can't *stand* this."

Harry gave her one of what had been many hugs, "I called the Governor at Pentonville. Told him what was happening."

"And?"

"If the photograph fits – he'll take my authority to stop the execution. Timms can call up to the very last second – he'll be right by the phone."

Kat nodded, understanding.

There was nothing more they could do.

KAT STOOD BY the window. She had decided to force herself to *not* look at the clock anymore. It was no friend, but rather a grim adversary mocking them every time the second hand went *click, click, click.*

Outside, she saw that the sky was already beginning to lighten. Dawn coming.

A life with barely minutes left to live.

The snow had kicked in again, and she thought how she had teased Harry about English winters versus the blizzards and Nor'Easters of New York.

Won't do that again, she thought.

And then, with the clock and Timms making the only noises, *there was another sound.*

134

A small buzz. And for Kat, a not unfamiliar sound. She was almost afraid to turn around and look at the machine.

But she did. As did Harry.

Both their breaths held.

Then the buzz was joined with the clackety noise of things inside the miraculous Telephotography machine… *working.*

They walked over to it.

WHILE KAT WANTED to go stand right in front of the machine to see what was about to be spewed out, she backed away, as an eager Loxley rose from his seat, planted himself there.

Timms had stirred, and now that he regarded himself as the leader of this *cutting-edge* investigation, had moved alongside Loxley.

The machine seemed to take forever to roll out what – even when only halfway printed – was clearly a face.

Another few tense moments and then Loxley reached out, seeming – Kat thought – to be almost hesitant to look at the photograph in his hand.

He took one glance then turned, with what could only be called the most relieved smile, and handed it to Kat. Harry at her shoulder looking down.

And all Kat could say was: *"And there he is…"*

It was a formal police identification photograph, but all the details came together…the narrowed eyes, the half-smile on the face, tell-tale wrinkles at the eyes suggesting someone who held a lot of secrets.

But no doubt at all.

The photo of this man who had killed before in Newcastle was that of the same man, sitting only yards away in a jail cell.

Will Davis – or whatever his real name was.

She saw Harry turn to the policeman in charge. "Sergeant Timms. Best we call London immediately."

Timms, his face grim with this revelation, nodded.

Harry put a hand on the stout sergeant's back.

"And since you may need help with that. Stopping things," Harry said, "I'll stay right here."

To which Kat added.

"And so will I."

She waited and watched as Timms dialled the number, which Harry had already handed to him.

The seconds ticking, ticking away…

"The Governor please, Sergeant Edgar Timms here, Mydworth Police."

Silence for a few more seconds.

Then: "The photograph came in, sir. It's Davis," said Timms. "No doubt about it."

Another pause, Timms staring at them, nodding, the phone to his ear.

"Thank you, sir," he said. "And a *very* good morning to you."

Then he put the phone down – and smiled.

"We *did* it!" he said.

And Kat forgave Timms the "we" – knowing that at the last second, Oliver Brown had been saved.

She turned and wrapped her arms around Harry.

20.

THE VALENTINE'S DAY BALL

KAT WATCHED HARRY return with two delicate glasses filled with a punch that Lavinia had simply pronounced as, *"Bit of this, bit of that – but quite pleasant."*

"Here you go, Lady Mortimer."

Kat took her glass and a sip. The band, a lively group of musicians who were playing all the hits of the day – from the West End to even the latest from the States – were on a break.

She clinked her glass against Harry's and watched him look around the hall, festooned in pink and white, with giant paper hearts and coloured lights lining the walls.

"Must say, the committee did a bang-up job in our absence."

Kat smiled. "Looks wonderful. Magical, even."

At which point Lavinia appeared beside them.

"You *two*. You must be completely exhausted. And yes, Harry we could have used your decorating help but as you can see, we all managed."

Kat saw her husband grin at that.

"I will definitely be on duty for the take down."

"Wonderful."

Then Kat noticed a hesitancy in Aunt Lavinia as she took a step closer.

"Harry, this latest adventure of yours and Kat's – *well done*, I say."

"It wasn't easy, Aunt Lavinia, I admit."

Kat nodded. "We nearly lost Harry on the roof of that farm."

"But you know, I had – well – more than a few questions," said Lavinia.

"So, did we," Harry said. "Think we still may do, eh, Kat?"

Kat was curious what Lavinia was going to ask.

"What I don't really understand – I mean, just being a regular person and all that – is why this Davis man didn't just, one night, *steal* the stock? I mean – at the end, that's what he tried to do, didn't he?"

Harry looked at Kat.

"Aunt Lavinia, that had me thinking too. Then I realised. The stock was worthless not being in his name. A man like Davis would know all about forgeries. And he also must have known he could use it for a scam and still make a pretty penny."

"What a *fiend*."

Kat smiled at that. "Perfect word. You know, when they showed Davis the photo – with him knowing there was all this evidence connecting him to the other killing – he actually bragged about nearly getting away with it all."

"And the housekeeper, Connie? Her role?"

Kat nodded at that. "Gave Davis's knock-out pills to Jeremiah, but he told her they were vitamins. All the while, Davis took advantage so he could explore and steal. So she's blameless," Kat said.

"And we're guessing that those pills were probably used to put Oliver Brown out for the count on the night of the killing," Harry added.

"I just hope," Lavinia said, "that poor man is free soon. Really free. And Mydworth gets back to normal."

"Never thought you'd catch me saying this, Lavinia, but me too! Oh – look, they're coming back."

And Kat turned to see the band, "Lester Noble's Rascal Cats" take their position on the Town Hall stage.

"Oh, good. Music's about to start," Kat said. "Maybe," she said downing her punch, "I can get a dance out of your nephew now."

"Absolutely," said Harry.

And as soon as the band started in with a bouncy version of *"You're the Cream in My Coffee"*, Harry took the punch glasses, set them down on a nearby table, and wheeled Kat out to the dance floor.

IT WAS ON their third dance that Kat heard a commotion coming from the other end of the Town Hall.

People making noises, a crowd gathering.

The band stopped mid song.

"Harry, is something—?"

And she saw that Harry wore a smile. What he would undoubtedly call a "cheeky" one – and he stopped high-stepping the Charleston with Kat, as she turned towards the entrance to see…

Mabel Brown. And beside her – large as life, towering over his wife – Oliver Brown. People came up and clapped him on the back, some onlookers applauding, others cheering. Mabel Brown's smile – as big as could be.

Ollie held, in his powerful right arm, Elsie, who clapped gleefully along with the crowd.

But Kat saw that, despite all his well-wishers, *the newly freed man did not stop.*

Instead, he walked with his wife directly towards Harry and Kat.

Kat leaned into Harry.

"Pulled some strings to get him released today, did you?"

"*That I did.* Wasn't sure it would work, you know, bureaucracy and all." He took a breath. "Glad to see it did."

And then Oliver Brown and his family stood before them. He gave a big smile – but in his eyes was something deeper. That awareness of what might have been, and how the two people he now faced had been able to change it.

He stuck out his hand.

"Lady Mortimer, Sir Harry, I can't tell you how much—"

Ollie stopped. Looked at his wife. *Words* obviously not his forte.

Then with a firm grip, he shook Kat's hand, then Harry's, and uttered the simplest but truest words.

"Thank you, both."

NEXT IN THE SERIES:

SECRETS ON THE COTE D'AZUR

MYDWORTH MYSTERIES #8

Matthew Costello & Neil Richards

When Harry and Kat head south to the French Riviera, they look forward to dazzling parties, a shimmering sea, and wonderful food. But once they step off the legendary Paris-Nice train, Le Train Bleu, things start to be anything but restful.

Asked to assist in a dangerous case of blackmail — they soon find that the streets and alleyways of the Cote d'Azur hide not only cafes and bistros… but also secrets and danger of a most deadly sort.

ABOUT THE AUTHORS

Co-authors Neil Richards (based in the UK) and Matthew Costello (based in the US), have been writing together since the mid-90s, creating innovative television, games and best-selling books. Together, they have worked on major projects for the BBC, PBS, Disney Channel, Sony, ABC, Eidos, and Nintendo to name but a few.

Their transatlantic collaboration led to the globally best-selling mystery series, *Cherringham*, which has also been a top-seller as audiobooks read by Neil Dudgeon.

Mydworth Mysteries is their brand new series, set in 1929 Sussex, England, which takes readers back to a world where solving crimes was more difficult — but also sometimes a lot more fun.

Made in the USA
Las Vegas, NV
15 April 2022

47551753R00090